Praise for *The Rabbit Punch*

'This beautifully restrained novel is built largely upon words exchanged between a father and his son. In paring back the elements, Missiroli says all there is to say about their differences, their devotion to one another, the frailties they share. I entered instantly into their private language and the piercing clarity of these pages, utterly absorbed'
Jhumpa Lahiri, author of *Interpreter of Maladies*

'For half a century the wintry charms of Rimini have been celebrated by the solitary voice of its most famous son, Federico Fellini. Now the arrival of Marco Missiroli has gifted us with a new perspective. Less dreamy and poetic, more embittered and down-to-earth – but equally hypnotic, and equally filled with unforgettable characters'
Sandro Veronesi, internationally bestselling author of *The Hummingbird*

'An intense, moving book – full of life, suspended between utter joy and pain, human errors and moments of pure redemption'
Domenico Starnone, award-winning author of *Tricks*

Marco Missiroli's first novel *Senza Coda* won the
Campiello Opera Prima (the Italian equivalent of the Costa
First Novel Award). Published to great acclaim, *Devotion*
(previously entitled *Fidelity*) was a number one bestseller
in Italy, was shortlisted for the Premio Strega (the Italian
Booker) and was made into a hit Netflix limited series.
Born in Rimini, on the Adriatic coast,
Marco now lives in Milan.

Also by Marco Missiroli

Devotion

Geoffrey Brock is an American poet and translator.
He is the author of three books of poems, the editor of
The FSG Book of Twentieth-Century Italian Poetry, and
the translator of books by Umberto Eco, Italo Calvino
and Roberto Calasso, among others.

The Rabbit Punch

Marco Missiroli

Translated by Geoffrey Brock

Sceptre

First published in Great Britain in 2025 by Sceptre
An imprint of Hodder & Stoughton Limited
An Hachette UK company

The authorised representative in the EEA is Hachette Ireland, 8 Castlecourt
Centre, Dublin 15, D15 XTP3, Ireland (email: info@hbgi.ie)

1

A CIP catalogue record for this title is available from the British Library

Hardback ISBN 9781399724012
Trade Paperback ISBN 9781399724029
ebook ISBN 9781399724036

Typeset in Sabon MT by Manipal Technologies Limited

Printed and bound in Great Britain by Clays Ltd, Elcograf S.p.A.

Hodder & Stoughton policy is to use papers that are natural, renewable and recyclable
products and made from wood grown in sustainable forests. The logging and
manufacturing processes are expected to conform to the environmental
regulations of the country of origin.

Hodder & Stoughton Limited
Carmelite House
50 Victoria Embankment
London EC4Y 0DZ

www.sceptrebooks.co.uk

to Rimini
and to Claudio Cazzaniga
(1980–2020)

I live on what others don't know about me.

Peter Handke

June

I'm at the supermarket when he calls. When I answer he clears his throat but doesn't speak. I know he drives around at night in his Renault 5.

I ask if he's okay.

'Sorry to bother you,' he says.

'Stop it.'

He drags on his cigarette. 'They pay you yet?'

'Not yet.'

We're quiet like when I was a kid and would watch him fixing a socket, the dresser in the kitchen, the back gutter. His fingers light.

Then I tell him I'm coming to see him.

'Really?'

'It's your birthday.'

'But how will you manage with work?'

'I'll manage.'

Five days later I arrive at his house in Rimini. The roller blinds are lowered and the garage door is wide open. He's among the tomato plants in his fisherman's cap.

'Hi,' he says, rising from the earth, shiny with sweat. 'Much traffic?'

'No, not much.'

He comes up beside me and reaches for my bag; I pull it away. I follow him into the downstairs apartment but stop as soon as we enter. Then he realises I want to sleep upstairs.

I raise the blinds in my old bedroom and the sun beats down on the dust and the shelf of Panini trading cards. Outside the window, the Renault 5 he has driven for twenty-seven years. One rim is dinged and the bumper is polished to a shine. It was Don Paolo who phoned me in Milan to warn me that he's been staying out until dawn and something's wrong.

'Wrong how?'

'Word at the bar is that he stops by at night with a scowl on his face. You know your dad.'

'Talk to him.'

'You talk to him, Sandro.'

Later he comes in with pillowcases and the rest. We make the bed, shaking the sheet out like she used to. We're slow and precise and as soon as we finish he leaves the room and heads to the kitchen.

I hear him rummaging, clattering, crunching. When I look in he's on his tiptoes on a chair browsing the preserves. He's developed a paunch.

He hops down, landing soft as a dragonfly, then goes to the stove and turns on the gas. Out of nowhere he whips out a match and the head flares: Nando the gunslinger.

Later I make my rounds. I walk up Via Magellano towards the Ina Casa housing complex, its windows packed with people waiting for June to come. And coming it is, the season's first outsiders bringing that acerbic cheer that those of us further from the beachfront find so tiresome.

It takes me until the park to shake Milan – it generally happens around the primary school or a little past, when I cut through the courtyard of the horseshoe building. My shoes loosen up and the North fades from my head as I reach the street that leads to Bar Zeta: I've come for the sea bream with the tuna-artichoke sauce. Someone says hello. Someone says: it's Pagliarani's son.

When I get home it's roasting hot outside and he's not in the kitchen. He's in my room checking the window screen. He signals that it's okay and goes out. He has cleaned up the nightstand, tidied the desk. My bag is still on the floor, the zip now a third of the way open.

We eat at 7.30 sharp and before we sit down he asks whether I've turned out the lights. What lights? The lights in the rooms you were in. He has a thing about waste, which he used to also take out on her: it's not like you're the electric company's wife, he'd say.

He stewed a local cockerel in a frying pan with potatoes, made a sauce with aubergine and squash flowers. He watches me suck the browned skin of the cockerel; he sucks it too.

'In Milan, you only eat frozen stuff.'

'Not true.'

'But you've got bags under your eyes.'

'And you're Clark Gable?'

Then he starts in again about the payments I'm expecting. He's ready to help me out.

'I'm good and anyway they're coming.'

'Still ten thousand eight?'

'Ten thousand four.'

'But how does that happen, at forty years of age.'

'I'm sorry I ever told you.'

He snorts. 'Sure you don't need anything?'

'I'm good.'

He pushes some crumbs around, cuts an aubergine stem and leaves it there. 'You give up your steady job and look what happens.' He springs to his feet and takes the wine from the sideboard, twists the cork out in one motion, rolls it between his fingers. 'When we shut down Bar America, remember how I was always yelling?'

'I remember you were always pissed off.'

'Five years earlier I'd lent fourteen million lire to Roberti who wouldn't pay me back and I needed it for the bar.' He pushes the squash flowers towards me.

'What's that got to do with my money?'

'It's got to do with it because I never had the guts to go and take those fourteen million back. Do you think I was calling Roberti about that? Not a chance.' He wipes his mouth. 'I was sitting at the table balancing the books every night. You call these guys?'

I nod.

He refills my wine. 'One Bar America is enough, Sandrin.' He lifts his glass. 'Cheers.'

But I know it's not Bar America. It's the crate of cardinal peaches. The trajectory that alters as he picks them with his father. He's fifteen, about to enrol in the surveying school in Ravenna.

She's the one I heard the story from. She told me as we climbed up to Verucchio, hand on her hip, her dancer calves out of tune with her mother body. She slowed to speak, winded: You, Muccio, choose the university you like and don't be like Dad in the peach orchard in San Zaccaria.

We paused to look out at the Marecchia Valley, beyond the city walls.

You know, that big orchard in San Zaccaria? So your dad's there with Grandpa Giuliano and he's about to settle on his new school. He's happy, he likes building sites, foundations, spirit levels and square metres – he thinks about that stuff even when he's arranging peaches in crates.

I was about to pass her and she grabbed on to my shirt, so I grabbed her arm and started to pull her, but instead she surged forward, pulling me.

So, at some point in the orchard your dad picks up a crate heaped with peaches and gets your grandpa to help him load it on to the cart by the ditch. That's where the road is, and just then Russi the engineer passes by. He greets your grandpa, your dad, asks how things are going, then notices the cardinals: those good? Your grandpa motions for him to try for himself, and Russi holds out a hand to catch one. But guess who throws him the peach over the ditch? Your dad. A beautiful toss. You know your dad, always throwing things with that perfect aim. Russi asks him if he wants to be a baseball player, then he takes a bite of the peach. As he chews, he learns that your father wants to be a surveyor. Russi takes another bite and looks at your grandpa: surveyor is no good anymore, nowadays you need to be an electronics expert. Electronics expert? Electronics and telecommunications, there's a school in Cesena, in Italy these days everybody's a surveyor. Then he throws his pit into the ditch, waves goodbye and goes on his way. Your grandpa leans over the crate, arranging the peaches even though they're already arranged.

And then?

We were about to finish the climb to Verucchio.

Well, by then your dad had already bought the rulers and the squares and the graph paper. But after the cardinal peaches he threw all that away.

We clear the table with the news on. He makes two instant coffees and adds milk. He hands me one and rubs his eyes. He has the chest of a swimmer and the hips of a girl. And that moustache. He wants to look like Volonté in *A Fistful of Dollars* but looks instead like D'Alema in parliament. He downs his heart pills and snatches up the briscola deck from the wicker basket. 'Let's play.'

I sip my coffee.

'We playing or not?' He hacks up some phlegm to clear his voice.

'I've got stuff to do.'

'A quick game,' he says, shuffling. He puts on his glasses, lights a cigarette and deals me the three cards.

I wait to pick them up. I'm looking at him and he's looking back.

'A quick one, Sandro, that's it.'

We play. On the third hand he takes my king of coins with his three of coins and his mouth widens like a frog's. 'Good times tonight,' he sneers.

'And other nights not so much?'

He snuffs his cigarette in the ashtray. 'Yesterday they showed Scorsese, *Goodfellas*. Remember that scene with the waiter with the bandaged foot and Pesci's shooting at him?' He draws a card and adds it to the others in his hand. 'And you, what do you do in the evenings?'

I draw a card too, my fingertips dry. 'I work, go out. Like that.'

'You still think about Giulia?'

I take his knight of swords with my three.

Electronics and telecommunications expert, ticket taker on seaside tour buses, railway worker, bartender, computer programmer for the railway. On his government ID he never chose to write: dancer.

After briscola we go out on to the terrace and I smoke too. Here I make him play a game: where would you want to be if you were a million euros richer and fifty years younger.

He sets his cigarette in the pot of geraniums and stands there sniffing the breeze from Ina Casa, which smells like the river. He answers at once: 'With my dad, working in the field. Or at that dance hall in Milano Marittima, with your mum.'

But you can tell already he's back with his father before he died, hacking clods.

'And you?'

'Fifty years is tough.'

'Twenty-five.'

I'm thinking I don't want to go back to being fifteen: those freckles, and Rimini's hard on shy kids. 'I want to be in London, in a penthouse apartment, watching people down on the street.'

'And the million euros?'

'The penthouse apartment.'

He gives me his squinty, puzzled look. He blows out smoke and blurts that there's a problem with the rules of my game: 'It makes no sense to ask what I would've bought fifty years ago with a million euros, which would have been a couple billion lire. It's better to ask: where would you want to be and what would you want to buy *now* if you were fifty years younger and a million euros richer.'

'Okay, go.'

He doesn't answer. He leans out from the terrace and studies the blackbirds scrabbling in the street. It's already summer at Ina Casa: loud voices from the balconies, playful shrieks from the courtyards. He's not talking anymore, he's smoking, his back to me. He always turns his back when he wants to be alone.

'Think about the million to spend now,' I say, resting a hand between his shoulder blades before going off to my room.

I turn on my computer. On the desk, the gooseneck lamp, old invoices, the box with my graduation-gift fountain pen. I uncap it, write in my diary to call the bank back about the line of credit, and then get down to work.

Forty minutes later, the Renault 5 starts up and drives off.

He took her paintings down. Her evening gowns are still here, and her shoes. And the safe, behind the last two volumes of the Fabbri encyclopaedia.

I unpack my bag: four T-shirts, a cotton sweater, two button-downs, a pair of sandals, three pairs of trousers. I zip it shut and arrange everything in my wardrobe. Nagged by the thought that he may have done what he did when I was a teenager: rifled through my book bags, the pockets of my clothes. Looking for evidence to confirm his suspicions.

It's past midnight when I stop working. He's still out. In the kitchen, the saucepan sits on the stove with a finger of milk, the matchbox on the scale. He left chickpeas soaking with bay leaves, beside a jug ready to pour the oil. I eat a slice of Emmental cheese, his favourite, which he cuts by slaloming from hole to hole. The briscola deck is sitting on the walnuts, in the wicker basket, strangled with a rubber band, next to a standard fifty-two-card deck. Outside, Via Mengoni is black.

I take the standard deck. I pick it up with my right hand and pass it to my left. I sit down and remove the rubber band. I scramble the deck and hold my fingers over the scattered cards. I gather them up. I do a riffle shuffle. The middle phalanx of my index finger always pushes against the back of the deck. I do a Hindu shuffle. Thumb plucking from the top, palm cupped. I slow down when my fingertips feel a bite. I spread the cards into a half moon, pick them up, repeat. Speed matters less than care: the tilt of the arm, the rotation of the wrist, the three middle fingers orchestrating. Since I first started doing this, I've been meticulous about it.

I start again then wrap up. I press the cards to the table with my palm. Their rustle is a gust through leaves, a flutter of goldfinch wings.

He returns at 3.20 in the morning. The front door clicks and footsteps ascend. I toss in bed with two thoughts:

either he has insomnia or – or what? For years instead of sleeping he haunted the living room, did I don't know what else. Apart from dancing he was never a very physical man.

I wait for him to go to his room but he doesn't. I hear the mumble of a car on Via Magellano, the groan of my bed, the emptiness of the room. I get up and join him in the kitchen.

He's sitting, a wake of smoke rising from the ashtray. He's wearing his good suit.

'Hey.'

'Hey.'

Then he says he thought about our game: who cares about the fifty years younger and the million richer. He wants to go back to Christmas 2009: the Grand Gala at the Baia Imperiale, overlooking Gabicce beach.

I drink a glass of water and say goodnight.

I'm sixteen when he finds me in the shed with a cigarette in my mouth. He asks how long that's been going on. Not long, I say, but he already knows I'm a liar.

'What do you smoke?'

'Marlboros.'

'How many?'

'One or two. Three on Saturdays.'

'Don't let your mum catch you. Promise me.'

Promise me: how good that pleading sounded in his mouth.

For lunch he makes rigatoni with tomatoes from the garden, and woe unto him who questions the portion size: a hundred and sixty grams for two. I come up behind him and add three rigatoni to the scale.

'Nitwit,' he says, but doesn't take them off.

He stirs the tomatoes on the stove, adding ingredients from his copper pots. He lights two matches, stoops to check the burners, wipes his brow.

He calls it his retirement recipe, dating from when he was forced out of the railway after coming home that afternoon in 1997.

I was translating Latin in the kitchen when he came in, drank some water with a hand on his belly, then went to lie down in his room. I didn't think much of it and kept translating, but when I checked on him I found him sleeping on his side, not snoring. I retraced my steps and called the doctor. Forty minutes had passed by the time he came to examine him, put a pill under his tongue and called the hospital. She – back when we all still lived in that house – raced home from school: Nando darling, and the caress she usually reserved for me.

Transmural myocardial infarction – at age fifty he was done with work.

The rabbit punch: among countryfolk, it's the blow to the nape that stuns the animal so they can skin it. In boxing, it's a punch to the back of the head. At the card table, it's when you have your back to the wall and pull off a big bluff.

'Were people out last night?' I fork up a piece of rigatoni and chew.

He shakes his head, barely touching his pasta. Suddenly he remembers he needs to check the garden to see if the red spider mites have come.

'The fuck is a red spider mite?'

'Tomato pest.'

'And you did the planting?'

'It was cabbage and squash's turn. But no.'

'No what?'

'A n ò vòja,' he said in Romagnolo.

'And what is it you do feel like doing?'

'A n ò vòja.'

After lunch I retire to my room, and soon I hear him rummaging in the dirt. He's hunched over like a woman in a rice paddy, with his fisherman's cap and his way of bending down and rising back up. A great dancer, she used to say. Everyone said so.

Later that afternoon I go out to get a birthday cake. I pedal to the beach, already blooming with umbrellas and burnt faces. In June, Rimini still belongs to Rimini: everyone knows each other and the sand is free of commotion.

I walk my bike through the big piazza in front of the Grand Hotel. We used to race animal-head tricycles under these pines – I always wanted the elephant. She watched from the racetrack fence, ice cream in hand, he stood behind her smoking.

Even back then Saint Honoré cakes were the only desserts he craved. I buy one that serves six, hide it in the downstairs fridge. I forgot candles. I look around, find two little pink ones in the desk drawer. The good suit he wore the other night is hanging from the wardrobe door handle. He ironed it.

Before dark I find an e-mail confirming my line-of-credit appointment. They also want to clarify my income records. I put my phone away and join him, tell him it's my turn to cook: a frittata with onions and courgette.

'Thanks,' he says.

'I should have blanched the onions.'

'Thanks for coming.'

'It's nice here.'

Neither of us is very hungry and we turn on the TV, which has good news about the financial markets. He asks if I have any updates about the payments I'm owed: I don't and he makes a peeved gesture with a toothpick in his mouth. Then there's a piece on the French Open, and we trot out memories of going to Rome for the Italian Open, perching on centre court, his Nadal and my Federer, salami sandwiches we'll finish on the train ride home.

'You'll be seventy-two tomorrow, Nando.'

'Big deal.' And he clears the dishes.

Around midnight the Renault 5 leaves the courtyard. The suit is missing from the study, the briscola deck is fanned out in the kitchen.

One Sunday in Milan I was with Giulia in Parco Sempione when he called to ask if Mum read the future using the pyramid or fan spread.

'You're not starting too.'

'Just curious.'

'And you can't ask her?'

'She says then I'll believe in it.'

'Fan and pyramid, both. Depends on whether you're asking about love or something else.'

Giulia laughed: we already had plans to move to Lisbon, get a house of our own.

But I had unknown houses and their tables. When I went in I would look for reassurance in a piece of furniture, a curio, a glimpse from the windows. We call it deflecting. As if we need to deflect the solemnity of the moment, distracting the bad luck.

It's best to find it in the first few minutes. The eye chooses a painting on the wall, a bottle opener, a pack of cigarettes, the chandelier. Objects. Never bodies. Bodies you look at to understand their moves. Bodies only when the game is on.

The next morning he's having breakfast on his feet – tea and fruitcake. He dunks, lets it drip before eating it. He clears his moustache with his bottom lip. Then he dissolves a sachet of pain relief powder in water. 'My old-man back.'

'Nando?'

'Yeah.'

'Happy birthday.'

I pat him on the shoulder, he drinks the pain medicine.

'I planned a little celebration.'

He looks at me sideways. 'I'm going to Montescudo.'

'I'll come.'

'You'll come?'

I don't remember which branch he was perched on the afternoon of the heart attack. Maybe the lowest, stoutest one. I lever my foot, hoist myself up and look down. He must have fallen between the trunk and the first weeds. Then he woke up and drove to Rimini.

From here our farmhouse in Montescudo looks like a stone box: a ruin he bought for a hundred and thirty million lire in 1993 and pieced back together himself. If he'd died, we would have buried him on this land. And what would he have missed? My graduation, her painting exhibition, me and Enrica naked in my bedroom and him coming in because we'd forgotten to lock the door, my first commercial, that big Christmas gala at the Baia Imperiale, the discovery of my vice, all those tomatoes.

Physical changes during the game: digits more activated, precise, with increased prehensility. Pupil mobility. Control of the cardiovascular system over the medium and long term. Almost an evolutionary process, observable within a few months of beginning play. And the players' haphazard but settled postures, each a talisman.

They started dancing again seven months after his heart attack. She's the one who tells me.

'Look, at the hospital they said to take it easy.'

'Your dad's in fine shape in the mornings.'

'You've been dancing at home?'

'In bed.' She was still blonde and used to call me at university every Wednesday.

'I don't want to hear that stuff!'

'Your dad was afraid his bypasses would pop out.'

'I don't want to hear that!'

'Muccio!'

'I swear I'm about to hang up.'

She's laughing.

'Keep laughing.'

'Imagine the headlines if it went badly: Nando Pagliarani, dead of love.'

We're cutting the grass at the bottom of the hill in Montescudo: I do most of it with the strimmer and he does the finishing touches with the scythe. He's shirtless, the toes of his shoes pressing into the ground, his upper body twisting with incredible torque. He masters the blade, lats bulging from his back. He bends over the gnarled tufts, tears at them with a fist. Belly jutting, collar bones protruding from his neck. He drops the scythe and wipes his forehead, stares at me.

I turn off the strimmer. 'What?'

'I'm giving myself a birthday present.'

'A new car.'

'A stone from the ruined church. I'll pull an animal out of it.'

We finish the grass and head for the church. Halfway there he passes me then slows to sniff the wild air. He's breathing hard and crouches over a dandelion, scatters it and becomes a bloodhound, his nose catching the wind from the hillside.

The church is fifty steps away. The belfry is crumbling and beneath it is a pyramid of rubble. The bloodhound rummages, selects a long stone. He sees a turtle in it, with a narrow shell. He starts to hoist it up but suddenly drops it and sits down, pressing his head and touching his back.

'Whoa there.' I bend over him.

'I'm okay, I'm okay.' He's listing to one side, his shirt half untucked from his Bermudas and billowing in the wind. His calves are sticks in his Nike socks.

I decide we need to go home right away. He protests, then follows because I'm carrying the stone. He tries to help, I shoo him away, and he passes me.

Have his legs always been so spindly? They march downhill, slowing and contracting over potholes, darting uphill, slicing through the wind. He's strong again. When he notices he's left me behind, he reverses course and finds me standing still, rock on the ground.

'Sandro?'

'You gave me an idea for an ad.'

'I did?'

I explain.

He considers. 'So, a gardener with a Nike wristband. A postman with a Nike jacket. A woman in labour at the hospital with her back—'

'Her ankles.'

'A woman in labour at the hospital with her ankles up on footrests, pushing.'

'And she has Nike socks on.'

He looks at his feet. 'How's it end?'

'Everything is sport.'

'Everything is sport.' He starts walking. 'Anyway they won't pay you.' He laughs his rich laugh.

We hide the stone in the ivy next to the tool shed and cover it with the overturned wheelbarrow. I ask him how he's feeling.

'I'm fine.' He stretches and then closes the farmhouse up. He does it quickly and dashes to the driver's seat of my car. He wants to drive. In a hurry to get back to Rimini, he opens the throttle until, about a third of the way, at Trarivi, he pulls over and gets out. He enters the yard of a farmhouse and five minutes later returns with a package in yellow paper: he says it's a nice surprise.

Mine's in the downstairs fridge. I take it out while he slips into the shower: the Saint Honoré has stiffened a bit and I plan to let it sit for at least half an hour before giving it to him. But as soon as I come back up he tells me he'll be going out shortly.

'Again tonight?' I sound like he did when I was a teenager.

'First we eat the nice surprise.' In his bathrobe he fetches and opens the yellow paper package: a pigeon. He puts it in a pan and sends me outside for some rosemary.

He planted it at the edge of the garden, where the earth crusts over in the garbino – the southerly wind that blows in from the Adriatic – and everything darkens in the light. Here the heat rises from below and bakes your ankles. Beyond, the shadowy paving slabs on which the Renault 5 sits. It's gleaming, even the wheels.

I go over, open the door – the lock button is always up – and get in. It smells clean. On the back seat, his roadside emergency kit and the cushion with bells sewn on the corners. From the mirror hangs the corded bracelet she had blessed at the church in Montefiore Conca. He refused to wear it but said nothing when he found it hanging from the rearview.

Trarivi pigeon, roasted Rimini peppers and a Spadarolo Sangiovese. The birthday menu. When cake time comes, I get up from the table, telling him I'll be right back so don't move.

He's itching to leave. I go down and take the Saint Honoré out of its box, plant a candle at the centre. When I go back up he's washing the dishes.

'No,' he protests.

I set the Saint Honoré on the table, light the candle.

'It's pink.'

'Go on, make a wish,' I say, and start singing happy birthday. He comes over, waving for me to stop, but he's happy because his eyes are big. He blows it out and pauses, lost in thought.

Half an hour later I'm writing about the woman in labour in her Nike socks when the Renault 5 leaves the gate. I feel uneasy – I don't know whether to call it a premonition.

Her, speaking about me: my son is a witch. She had a thing about Gustavo Rol and prophecies. After she died, he threw out all her books on oracles and locked himself in the kitchen. Then in September I found him behind the house hoeing up the old lawn.

'What's this?'

'A garden.'

The appearance of anomalies in daily life. The elation, if you're planning to play. The gloom, if you're not. Wrist tremors, leg tremors. The sense of alertness and sudden drowsiness. Living by the mathematics of winning and losing: everything as addition or subtraction. Feasting, fasting.

I fall asleep and don't hear him come back in. The next morning he's in the kitchen making a cold chickpea soup. If he's cooking early it means he's in a good mood. He tells me he had breakfast with Saint Honoré. I open the fridge: he scarfed down a cream puff without touching the rest.

'You ate it last night.'

'At night only Emmental.' He lifts the lid from the pot and breathes in the savoury steam.

He's definitely feeling good, I can tell by his quick movements, and so am I. Maybe we're feeling like we did in Sardinia in 1998, the year we finally learned the Adriatic wasn't everywhere.

That August we'd wake up at seven and make everyone breakfast before it got hot. Lunches and dinners too, and apple fritters, and sauces, and loaves of bread stuffed on the fly. For Mum and Patrizia and that Riccione couple we fell out of touch with. I must have been twenty, at university in Bologna, and he was retired. I remember how content we were in the kitchen of that rented cottage.

Then came the ninth day of our holiday: I left the beach early and climbed up a path that led straight to the house. I went that way to skip two hairpin bends of the winding trail, and I paused at the stone boundary wall to shake the sand from my slides, then stepped over it and climbed the outside stairs that led to the upper floor. That afternoon, however, I could hear the outside shower, which was set into the wall, hidden from the path. A slow gurgling sound. I kept going and saw that it was Patrizia, my mum's friend. Her bathing suit pulled down to her navel.

I stood and stared: her tanned body, the soap, her trying to hurry, the bronze nipples, her gaze on me. At first she seemed startled, then she smiled and carried on soaping up.

I stepped back and to one side. Patrizia lowered her swimsuit even more as she rinsed, then turned off the water, wrapped her body in a towel and her hair in a turban, and went back inside. I followed her with my eyes as she disappeared behind glass doors, feeling emboldened to take some action, but what – run after her, and then?

I turned, either to make my move or to retreat, and saw him: Nando. I froze, then slipped away, head bowed, without a word. Even later we never spoke about it, except on the last night when we were having a farewell barbecue and Patrizia appeared in a skimpy floral dress. Stirring the coals, he looked at me and whispered, be good.

I confided everything to him without confiding anything. As a kid I'd have conversations with him in my head and immediately hope to detect a reaction from him: an arched eyebrow, a drumming of fingers, a complicit smirk as if he'd heard me telepathically.

And my happiness in those hours when I'd follow him around as he performed tasks I could watch: unclogging a sink, pruning the roses, cleaning the inside of the car. Spells cast by his hands.

'I know what I'd do with the million from our game.' His chickpea soup half finished, he pushes the bowl aside and goes to the window. Opens it wide. 'First, build a veranda on the west side of the Montescudo house. And a pool at the edge of the field, made of stone and wood and with an electric cover. A heated pool because it's in the shade half the day.'

'That leaves you about nine hundred thousand euros.'

'I'll buy a guy to follow you around and turn off the lights you leave on.'

'Be serious.'

'Fine, I'll tell you.' He sits back, crossing his legs and lighting a cigarette. 'I'll get a new car.'

'But you won't even get a new radio for the Renault 5.'

'You can only have good music in the house.'

'What kind then?'

'I'll buy a Dacia Duster LPG.'

'No way.'

'Yep.'

'Why haven't you bought one, then?'

'The Renault still runs,' he says, taking a puff and then getting up to fiddle with his grocery notepad and add something to the list. 'We need oregano and anchovies. We can make pizza.'

'I'll take you out. Let's go to La Brocca or that place in Rivabella.'

'How much have I got left, in that game of ours?'

I bum a cigarette from him. 'After the Dacia Duster, about eight hundred and eighty grand.'

'I'll give it some thought.'

After dinner he campaigns for briscola again. While I make coffee he goes to fetch the deck and is standing there watching as I add a spot of milk. We decide to play five games.

We're at two all when I take his three of trumps with my ace. He's annoyed, has taken out two cigarettes, and wants to let off steam by grazing on the Saint Honoré: I know because he's staring at the fridge door. Then he has a fit of insistent coughing, clutches his chest and goes to the cupboard for his syrup. He takes a gulp and licks off his lips.

'I've been thinking,' he says, calmer. 'I've still got eight hundred grand and change, right?'

'Right.'

'I'll buy a cabin in the mountains, in Pozza di Fassa. And use the rest to hire the real Tina Turner to sing in my living room.'

We laugh, his mobile phone rings, we keep laughing, and he doesn't answer in time: it was Don Paolo. Before he was a priest, they were classmates. He calls him back and they talk about this and that and at the end of the chat Paolo wants to talk to me, as he does whenever I'm around. He asks how I think Nando is doing.

I go to my room and say he seems normal.

'Normal, you say,' and he meditates on that. He has a law degree and legend has it he was Prime Minister Andreotti's confessor. 'He was also normal on his wedding day, Sandro.'

This, too, is legend: Nando deciding to tear down the mouldy wall of the little kitchen two hours before marrying her at the city hall.

After dinner I'm the one who goes out: I've arranged to meet my friends at Walter's place, which is having its summer opening. It used to be a watermelon stand and now it's a bistro – Gradella – with a leafy terrace over-looking the canal.

I arrive with twenty euros and no debit card, and everyone's there. Some have never left Rimini, one's an actor in Rome, one a doctor in Bologna. We meet at Christmas and sporadically during the year.

'The Milanese who comes and goes,' they tease.

'I'm staying this time.'

'Half a day?'

'Depends whether Nando wants me around.'

Even with them I call him by name, as if he were one of the gang and might show up at any moment. They make room for me at the table, and Lele hands me a skewer of roasted meat. I know we won't lose track of each other. Though there was a time, with university, all of us going our separate ways, made timid by our small town . . .

I order a beer and look out over the canal. Seagulls gliding and boats coming in. Gatherings in front of the houses of Borgo San Giuliano, clothes rippling in the breeze. And I think: it's four years now he's been without her.

We all order another beer, and Lele and I drink ours on the little wall by the canal. I tell him Nando's been sneaking off like a thief in the Renault 5 and coming back in the middle of the night. He stares at me; he's an actor but has a May-I? face. He ponders: in his view, he goes for drives just to be driving.

'Just to be driving.'

'Yeah.'

'For months now?'

'How do you know it's been months?'

'They told Don Paolo at the bar.'

'Can't mind their own fucking business.'

Mosquitoes nip the water and dusk swallows the prows. Lele won't get remarried either – the theatre always keeps him on the move, and that's that. I ask him how long he'll stay in Rimini.

'Until the next audition. You?'

'I'd planned to leave today.'

'Then why aren't you leaving?'

'What are you, the Gestapo?'

He buttons his shirt cuffs and turns up his collar because he wants to be Alain Delon, and I tell him so.

'Fuck you and Delon both.' Then, seriously: 'Or rather, Bruni.'

'What?'

'Steer clear.'

'Don't start.'

'I don't like it when you stay longer than expected in Rimini.'

'Don't start.'

'I'll say it again: Bruni.'

'What if I don't have his number anymore.'

'What if you do.'

'You're both dicks.'

'You know he even deleted his Facebook.'

'So what?'

'Or so I hear.'

'Whatever.'

'Anyway, Bruni took himself out of circulation, Sandro.'

I finish my beer and rest my elbows on the wall.

'A few more days in Rimini – I'll be fine.'

'Then you should meet Bibi this time.'

'Bibi again.'

'She's a biologist. Thirty-two, Milan connections. Her name says it all: Beatrice Giacometti.'

'Rich?'

'Not at all.'

'Jewish?'

'Not at all.'

'Tits?'

'Normal.'

'So why are you trying to set us up!'

'Because this one'll smack you in the face if you don't behave yourself.'

I get home late and a bit tipsy. The Renault 5 is in the courtyard, the light in his room is on. I picked up three cream puffs at Bar Zeta and I eat one in the kitchen while checking out Beatrice Giacometti's Instagram. Private profile, tiny picture: brunette, Roman nose, mischievous eyes. Bibi.

I leave two cream puffs on a plate for breakfast, cover them with a paper towel, then go upstairs. The door to his room is ajar.

He calls me in. He's reading and the lampshade leaves his face dark. He takes off his glasses. 'So, we'll go for pizza?'

'The Rivabella place is good.'

'I'm in the mood for a capricciosa.' In his hand, one of the Simenon mysteries he's been reading all his life.

'You and your endless Maigret.'

'I liked him better on TV.'

26

I say goodnight and it occurs to me that I don't read anymore – it's the first thing to go when the thoughts set in.

A kind of tensing of the spine. Or: a tingling of the scalp. Or: an icy gust on the nape. My bad premonitions. They'd come as soon as I sat down at the table. And when they did: never touch the deck first.

I loaf all morning. He's in the garden for the endive though rain is coming: hunched over, digging and kneading new soil into old – with an open hand, a fist, a single finger, three fingers – until the rain starts falling on his back. He stretches and crawls towards each little plant, pawing at roots to make leaves stand clear, and he harvests. He's mired in mud, rain blackening his blue shirt, the back of his head. He hunches over, stamps to flatten mounds, smooths them with his forearms, wipes dirt off his forehead, presses a palm to his side but keeps going. It's starting to storm and I call to him from the window.

He signals to me that he's coming, and he really is, fists wrapped around his crop. He stomps his heels on the door-mat and when he ascends into the house he's drenched and whistling Venditti.

The good premonition: not having any. Normalcy, the run of days without tremors. Smooth sailing until the cards come out.

I go to the bank in the early afternoon. It's the second line of credit I've applied for. They're optimistic that the additional income documents will satisfy management. They'll let me know soon.

As soon as I'm home I fake a phone call, with him listening in from the kitchen: Well, you could have told me you were about to send payment, I mean, why put people through all this? Seven months late, and be glad I haven't gone to a lawyer – just transfer it to me and be done with it.

I put my phone back in my pocket, go into the kitchen and find him baking apples. He pauses: 'Lorenzi the notary has good lawyers if you need them.'

'It's taken care of.'

'The ten thousand four hundred.'

'Almost all of it.'

'And apart from that, how're you doing?'

'I'm fine.'

'I mean for income.'

'College courses, in the autumn.'

'And till then?'

'I'm fine till then. You took the whole storm today, huh.'

Rai 1 is on the TV. He's moving away from the oven. 'Shall we go to the cemetery?'

It's still raining but he doesn't give a damn about getting wet. He strides out of the house and slips into the Renault 5. I take cover under my hands and follow.

We bolt away from Ina Casa, take Via Marecchiese out to Spadarolo, hitting the first hill just past the school. The Renault 5 shrieks under fifty, and when it goes faster we stick out the tips of our tongues in solidarity. The air is wet, the fields are full of wheat and poppies and mallow. On the back seat of the Renault, a bouquet of wildflowers. He picked them in Montescudo, he says, and kept them in water in the garage. I never saw them there.

We park by the wrought iron gate. He gets out first with the flowers and waits for me to fetch the umbrella from the boot. He crosses himself. We haven't been to the cemetery together since the funeral.

She's up a small stairway, in a columbarium with her parents. She's laughing in the photo, but warily.

He steps away from the umbrella and goes to the fountain to fill the watering can and returns. He removes the wilted flowers from the Montescudo bouquet, adjusts the rest, adds water and wipes her stone with a cloth. His motions are hurried. He takes a step back and stands at an angle as if ready to leave. Instead he goes to her and presses his fingers to the photo, speaks to her. But I can't hear what he says.

'And you, Sandrin? What do you do with your million?' He's smoking and cruising over the Spadarolo ridge – he clearly doesn't feel like going home. The sun is out and beating on the damp.

'I'll put one chunk in the bank' – I'm tilting my seat back – 'and the rest to London.'

'You and your London.'

'You've got Montescudo, I've got London.'

'But the Brits are kind of arseholes.'

'How would you know.'

'Londoners for sure.'

'The "nice industrialist" is from London.'

'But he knew he'd make money off you.'

'No, he didn't.'

We climb the bend towards Covignano Hill.

'I think they told the industrialist he'd make money off you.'

'Who did?'

'Dunno.'

'Then why talk?'

'I mean, this big cheese just opens his door to some kid from Rimini? Who talks to him about flamingos with prosthetics?'

'That's why he's a big cheese and you're—' I look out the window.

'I'm what?'

'Better if you don't talk.'

'And I'm what?'

'Like this – all of you.'

'All of who?'

'You, your generation.'

'What about us?'

'Stop it.'

'What are we like, my generation?'

'Stop talking.'

'The hell are we like?'

'Too bloody cautious.'

Now the hill is in shadow and he slows to let his eyes adjust. He puts out his cigarette. 'Flamingos with prosthetics. Go on, what was that idea you pitched to the big cheese in London?'

'No.'

'C'mon.'

'The cautious generation.'

'Cautious how?'

'Punch the clock at the railway and toe the line.'

'And what about you?'

'What about me?'

'You – what've you risked, Sandro?'

'More than you.'

'What've you done? Chosen a woman? Had a family? A mortgage?'

'Punch the clock at the railway and toe the line.'

'Oh right: you take risks with cards.'

'Let me out,' I say, slapping the window.

'Stop it.'

'Let me out!'

But he speeds up. He tucks his chin to his chest and grips the gearstick.

'Flamingos, tell me what that was like, c'mon. What was that idea you pitched to the big cheese in London?'

'Always a court case, both of you.'

'C'mon, what was it, let's not kill the mood.'

I steady my voice: 'We're all flamingos.'

'And there was this flamingo with a prosthesis instead of a raised leg,' he says as we pass the Paradiso, having gone further out of our way. We slow down to peek at the shuttered disco, its forgotten grounds. 'And what did the industrialist do as soon as he saw you in front of his house?'

'You know.'

'Can't remember.'

'He was standoffish. So I told him I had an idea for his agency.'

'Then what?'

'You know.'

'And then – c'mon c'mon.'

'Then he invited me in for coffee.'

'And six months later your mum was watching TV. She must have phoned fifty people, Sandro's ad is on tonight, Sandro's on television, she kept saying.' He adjusts the rearview. 'She always did that for you, Sandrin.'

'C'mon, let's go for a walk.'

We walk along the beach from Bagno 5 to Bagno 33, the locals impatiently awaiting the high season, in their tank tops and one-pieces, some already in the water even though the sea is still rough, having held back the storm. To the south, the tip of Gabicce juts clear and we insist on walking Romagnolo style, half rushed and half lazy, head high and knees strong. Until he stops still. He reaches for me with one hand and leans forward, holding on and being held: 'Sandro.'

'Is it your back?'

'Let's go home.'

'You're tired.'

He's ankle-deep in sand and sweating. I lean down and pull him to me, taking his arm, and we walk slowly back up the beach, haltingly because he doesn't want my help. Eventually we come off the sand and find a bench. I sit him down, mop his brow with my sleeve and tell him I'll get the car. And then I almost run, thinking of his heart attack on the cherry branch. My phone always on even at night, in Bologna and Milan, train schedules memorised, imagining her voice saying Come quick, come because your dad's ill.

When I get back to Bagno 33 he's watching the people walk by, hands limp on his lap. I wait for him to see me, but he doesn't, so I honk.

He turns around, lifts an arm.

For dinner, stuffed squid and cucumbers, a glass of wine. He doesn't want to go to bed. He nibbles, pushes his plate aside, and gets up; he fiddles with the shopping list, takes a licorice wheel from the pantry, then vanishes into his room and turns the TV on.

I retreat to my room too. I don't want to leave him alone but I'm in the mood for company. I call Lele, who's exhausted and already watching Netflix. I consider swinging by to see Walter at his bistro, then I give up and look for a movie among the surviving DVDs. I come across the documentary about Moroccan goats and argan trees. Seven, eight goats perched on the branches, eating shoots and posing like living Christmas ornaments. I put it on and ten minutes later hear his door open again. He goes back and forth between his study and the living room. Goes to the bathroom, then back to his study and into the hall, then back to his room for a while, then out into the hallway again, then down the stairs, clicking the front door open, then shut, his footsteps outside, the Renault 5 starting up.

I put on my shoes, grab my keys, and run down. The Renault 5 is already heading up Via Magellano. I get in my car and drive off after him, lose him then find him again: he's taken Via Marecchiese, and I realise I left the documentary on and it must have got to the part with the goats on the argan tree. I keep his Renault 5 at a distance, follow it around the Villaggio Azzurro to the south. But he was tired… I accelerate. But he must have needed to rest… I go faster and this time my uneasiness is a desire: a hope to find him with a friend, a girlfriend, his old good cheer.

The Renault 5 turns on to Via di Mezzo and pulls over. He gets out and slips into Bar Sergio, buys cigarettes at the till, then comes back with the pack in his left hand. He's wearing his shirt with the spearpoint collar.

He climbs in and drives off again, heading towards Marina Centro with its beach-gear shops that have swallowed up the newsstands, keeps going past Central Park and the Embassy, staying parallel to the beach and accelerating towards Piazza Tripoli, which as a boy made me think of Africa.

He parks in front of the church, and I park too. He gets out and walks towards the windowless building we used to eye, revving our motors, many summers ago: they held parish parties inside. In the early 2000s it became an arthouse cinema, but tonight there are no posters in the display cases and its neon sign – Atlantide – is unlit. A silver-haired woman standing guard at the door greets him, they chat in low voices, and he goes in.

I wait, get out of the car, approach. Music and amplified voices emerge from the cinema; the silver-haired woman prepares to greet me. I say hello and ask what movies are playing, and she tells me they haven't shown films since the beginning of June and it's members only.

'And you get the membership here?'

'At the Railway Social Club offices.'

The music is coming from below: country, country and western, something like that. The voices at the microphones break off, start in again.

34

'Thank you,' I say, turning away.

'Are you railway or ex-railway?'

I shake my head. 'Just asking,' I say, waving and heading around towards the back of the building. The windows are small and dark and the only light issues from three portholes at street level. The music is coming from there: a large room in the back where people are dancing. They have hats in their hands. Cowboy hats, in Romagna.

The chrysalis: the moment before a big bet. Posture tightens up, fingertips press down on the chips, thoughts vanish. You forget who you are.

We never had a cowboy hat in the house. Or did we?

Maybe she did, but not him. She was the one who first dragged him on to the dance floor but then he got a taste for it: black shirt tucked crisply into trousers, shoes gleaming. He'd give her a tango-style dip even when it didn't fit the dance, and they always closed with the Scirea Hop. The sight of them embarrassed me: the hint of sensuality, their audacious hands.

I prolong the return trip, look for songs on the radio, then switch it off. I make a U-turn, go back to the beachfront strip, and park near the Embassy: once a nightclub, now a restaurant. A little further on is Central Park, our arcade of choice as kids: the rapid-fire lights of the screens, the jingles of Double Dragon and Street Fighter, the clatter of metal in coin-push machines.

I go inside, get change for a fifty-euro note and head to the slots area. It's still the same, except the pinball machines in the entryway are gone.

I win twelve euros. Twenty-one more. I lose.

I leave to get change for another fifty, come back and go to the till. A girl is changing six euros for tokens, and the machine spits them out in tub number two. The clinking. The festive racket. The building up of a fortune. I want tokens too: I order twenty euros' worth. They give me my change and I wait for the jingling, the clattering, the building up: they all ring in the gears of the machine that leaks them into tub number one. Forty tokens, plus five for free. A handful and a half. I pick them up, squeeze them so they dig into my palm, squeak one against another, warm my skin. To gamble them, or not: to not gamble them and to keep the scalding metal on me, to leave this place, to squeeze my fingers tightly around them before getting back into the car and dumping them into my pockets. My full pockets.

Then to search my phone for Bruni's number – address book, old messages – knowing it's no longer there.

I'm thirteen when I slip my index finger into the drawer of their old coffee grinder to steal ten thousand lire. I spend it sparingly: a Dylan Dog comic, a skateboard magazine, Saturday afternoon pizza slices, Panini trading cards. I make it last, hoard leftover coins, portion out my little treasure according to a hierarchy of needs. It's good to be ready if your friends propose a pedal-boat outing, a beach umbrella rental, Best Company sweatshirts, the first Sunday afternoon discos. Eventually we start going to the Venusian, an arcade downtown, and buying tokens for three thousand lire, or sometimes five thousand because then you get more bonus ones.

The coffee grinder sits on the highest kitchen shelf, above the shelf with the grocery-list notepad and the recipe book; I stand on a chair to reach it. The small notes are on top. When I no longer need the chair I stand on tiptoe and start pilfering the fifty-thousands on the bottom. I pilfer once every four weeks, to supplement my allowance. Then every three. Then two. The arcade, the slots at Bar Sergio, the blackjack machines at the petrol station.

One day he tells me: 'Your hands have got longer.'

I say nothing. Two days later I check the grinder drawer and feel the cash still there. I pause, index finger against the curling notes, then pull back, afraid.

'I'll raise your allowance to a hundred thousand a month,' he says one Thursday. And she always slips me an extra ten or twenty thousand from her purse.

After Central Park I go home. I leave the car on Via Mengoni, go through the gate, climb the outside steps two at a time, forty-five tokens jingling in my pockets. I pause, feeling my loot. Forty-five tokens. I extend my fingers and curl them back up, extend and curl. This was always a sign: clammy hands, seams of sizzling flesh.

In the kitchen I turn on the sink light, crack open a beer, and sit down. I shuffle the briscola deck and deal the cards out in a pyramid: thirteen, the last one at the top. I've forgotten to cut so I start over.

'Does it work on yourself?' I asked her one evening as she was reading the cards to find out if her exhibition at the Grand Hotel would be a success.

'As long as you don't cross your legs.'

Every time Lele dates a woman he falls in love and wants to give up his acting career.

'My kingdom for each of them.'

'But you always break it off.'

'I get off the horse before I get thrown off.'

As kids we used to go to Laura's café, at Bagno 5, to spend money and talk shit. Him with his fanny pack and his banana. He was always broke, which he joked about, and while we ate our ice cream sandwiches he cheerfully peeled a Chiquita. Now we order iced coffees by the marina at Souvenir and sit at a table half in the sun.

Today he's thinking ahead, setting a cigarette on the table for when he finishes his coffee. It doesn't take him long, him with his knack for sizing me up, an Inspector Derrick of Romagna: the fact is that I am not convincing him at all.

'Not convincing you at all about what?'

'You know.'

'I don't.'

'That old business.'

'Enough already.'

He grabs my arm. 'So that look is because of your dad?'

'What look.'

'Sandro?' He doesn't let go of my arm.

'What, Daniele?'

'Is it the old business?'

I take out a cigarette too. 'The old business is sorted.'

The waiter delivers our iced coffees.

'How sorted?'

'Sorted.'

'And Bruni?'

'Again?'

'Wasn't it Bruni who got you started in Milan too?'

'What's that got to do with anything?'

'The temptation's still there and you know it.'

We drink our coffee, we light our cigarettes. 'Fact is I'm broke. I'm not getting paid. And Nando's glad for me to stay here.'

'How much do you need?'

I wave him off.

'I just want to be home for a while.'

On our Rivabella pizza night, before we go out, it hits me: the cowboy hat must be in the basement. I go down and find a bowler hat they wore one year for Carnival. There are cases of wine in the corner, and the grill and Allen keys and his chest of tools: screwdrivers, trowels and chisels, drills, epoxies, God knows what. He's added a fire extinguisher, left their cast-off clothes on hangers. I lean against the wall. I used to come here as a boy, close the folding door, with a torch and a stack of Tiramolla comics to page through – the first thrill of feeling hidden, invisible. And later, the pleasure of hearing them call out my name with worry.

He actually does order the capricciosa. He used to get the diavola and once went through a phase where he only ate sausage pizza.

'You're the only one who gets tuna pizza, Sandrin.'

'Moira Orfei ate a slice whenever she was feeling envious.'

He bursts out laughing. 'Is that true?'

'I think she said it in an interview.'

'You and Moira Orfei then.' We clink our beers and the hollows of his cheeks fill in. He's looking sharp in a blue button-down, sleeves rolled up. He dabs his moustache and I feel like talking.

He can tell. 'What's up?'

'Nothing.'

'What?'

I spread the napkin on my lap. 'You should have that fatigue checked out. I'll go with you.'

'I'm not sleeping well.' He looks towards the waiters.

But the pizza's not coming yet. We drink our beer and look out from the veranda. I asked for a table facing the Adriatic; the big umbrellas are closed except for two – the lull before the partiers. Certain evenings at this time, up until secondary school, we'd picnic on the beach: she'd bring pastries and we'd invite Lele and a few others, as the nightly beachfront promenade gathered steam, us still in our swim trunks.

'Remember how nice it used to be?' I ask.

'You always with the tuna and the hard-boiled eggs.'

Then the pizzas come, but we hold off eating until they bring the spicy oil. He puts some on mine: a few scattered drops.

As we stroll along the beachfront, I tell him that like Moira Orfei I too have an envy indicator. Mine's not a tuna pizza, but a toe. Every time I want something someone else has, my left big toe rears up.

'Just the left one?'

'Just the left.'

'Give me an example.'

'That washing machine commercial: the clothes in the drum that turned into fish in the ocean – the scarf that almost imperceptibly became a jellyfish. Remember?'

He doesn't.

'The first time I saw it I felt my big toe banging the top of my shoe.'

He lights a cigarette, offers me one and takes two puffs. 'So you're an envious person, you.'

'Sometimes, yeah.'

'Sorry, but what is it you haven't got?'

'That's not the point. You're envious because you want some random thing.'

'Random, in what sense?'

'Who knows.'

'A good woman?'

'For instance.'

'That penthouse in London.'

'Yeah.'

'The Oscar for commercials.'

'If only.'

'And what else?'

I wink at him. 'You know.'

He suddenly stops.

'Your vice.'

'C'mon, I'm kidding.'

But he's walking the other way, his gait jerky.

'C'mon, Nando, I was kidding.'

'No, you don't kid, you nitwit.' His cheeks are hollow again. 'So your envy is not for some random thing.'

'Let's hear it.'

'It's to have all of Sandro Pagliarani.' He stops. 'To have yourself as you are, bullshit included.'

I smoke, say nothing.

He tosses away his half-smoked cigarette. 'In the end I think we just want the two or three things we come into the world for.'

'Such a philosopher.'

'Such a nitwit.'

We start walking again, out of sync, Rimini listless around us. For the past twenty years we've waited until July for the ruckus that up until 2002 came in May. I ask if he feels like getting ice cream; he doesn't but as soon as I get one he's angling his face towards it, licking his lips.

'I guess I was envious when the Nicolinis bought that little farm.'

'Up in Santarcangelo.'

'Christ what a deal.'

'I hung out with Daniele the other day.'

'How's he?'

'On a break from touring.'

'I saw him in that TV series on Rai 1.'

He's not sure which way to go, so I pick up the pace and steer him towards Piazza Tripoli, slipping into the bustle that flows from Bounty to the piazza. There he dashes into a tobacconist's and comes out with a lighter, flicking it on and off for no reason. He's like a child, and I tell him so.

'Ah, youth. That one, yeah, a terrible envy.' Then we cross the square and come to the church. I finish my ice cream, throw away my napkin and stare at the Atlantide:

it's open, and the silver-haired woman is standing in the doorway.

'Shall we head back?' I ask.

'Let me show you something.'

He walks me over. He tells the silver-haired woman I'm his son and he wants to show me the party. She smiles, then we're inside on a landing. It's crowded, there's no music, jets of air conditioning on our necks. We go down about a hundred steps and spill into a large room. The dance floor is on the far side.

'This is it,' he says.

People crowd in behind us, most over fifty though a few are younger, all with cowboy hats in hand. He motions for me to follow him to the bar, where he talks to a young woman in a white shirt and black waistcoat.

'What would you like?' she asks me. 'Your dad's having a sambuca.'

'Sambuca's good, thanks.' I sit on a barstool.

He's half a metre away, handing money to the bartender, sitting down beside me. More people come in and the music starts and they move to the dance floor. It's country, country and western. I sip my sambuca. He leans in. 'This is it,' he repeats, 'after your mother.'

Eight seconds: the average time it takes a novice to reveal himself to other players, regarding the hand he has just been dealt.

His feet can't wait under his stool: his toes pivot and tap as he scans the room, eyeing the lights on the ceiling, the cowboys, me. I look towards the rear of the room, embarrassed, but when I look back he's still staring at me. I nod – yes, go – as if he's asked permission.

He finishes his sambuca, stands, readjusts his rolled-up shirt sleeves. He swings his hand, tilts his wrist, and I realise it's the same movement they're making on the dance floor with their hats in their hands. He tilts his head in the direction of the dancers, inviting me to join him.

'You go ahead.'

He walks off, over to a heavyset guy in jeans who's playing music from a console. He says something and the heavyset guy reaches under the table and brings up a stack of cowboy hats for him to choose from. He takes two, thanks the guy, and comes back over to me. 'Let's dance.'

But I don't dance. I stand there holding the hat – a John Wayne hat, with steel studs and cord around the crown.

And where is he? After waiting for the song to end, he walked down the aisle between the chairs, chest broad and calves taut, and lined up on the floor with the others. They arrange themselves in seven horizontal lines, ten or so dancers per line, roughly half a metre between them. The music starts again and he holds the crown of his hat hip-high, lifts it towards his face, then flips it over and puts it on.

Back straight, he claps his hands three times – everyone does, as they do full turns and realign themselves. They take their hats off and begin with one step forward and one step back, stamping their heels before a pirouette. He's serious, concentrating on his feet, then he laughs.

And he keeps laughing. Because that's him: John Wayne.

You have to play about six months and fifteen tables without causing any trouble to be accepted into the good circles. Then they say: you're in.

After I was in, up in Milan, they gave me a nickname: Rimini.

Outside the Atlantide I give him my jacket. He drapes it over his shoulders without putting his arms in the sleeves, and I push it up in the back to cover his neck. I imitate his pirouette and his hat-flip gesture.

He says: 'It's fun.'

It's a good sound in his mouth: *fun*, a rich tone, *fun*, Nando Pagliarani. I'm swallowing a lump in my throat; he can tell and asks if I'm okay.

Fun. I've waited years to hear him say that.

They used to do the boogie-woogie, they danced to sixties songs and mazurkas, they slow danced. They danced to Queen and Daft Punk, to Secondo Casadei. They entered shag dance competitions. Autumn, winter, spring, summer. But their prime dance time was the month after the last beach umbrella closed, with Rimini still keyed up and jackets freshly fished from wardrobes. Then they would wear their feet out. They'd put on records as soon as they got up and gather strength until dusk, heels and soles clacking in rooms around the house, in the garage, calves flexed and arms flailing, and when evening came they'd hit the dance floors until the small hours. They'd come home looking like a mess, clothes rumpled and collars askew. As well as grumpy, evasive, distracted. Nando and Caterina and their off-season. Their scaramàz, as she called it.

'Scaramàz?'

'Setting the soul on fire, Muccio.'

Eventually the record player would return to normal and they'd both go back to looking after things. At most she might sway her hips to some TV song, or he might let loose a leg or foot in the hall – a quick flurry of tapping, a hint of the Scirea Hop. But never country.

And Tuesdays, when she had her evening painting class and he would stew on the sofa as he waited for her. What did you paint, he'd snap as soon as she walked in. A still life. Oh, a still life. And he'd glare at her as she took off her amethyst earrings in the bathroom.

He keeps the earrings on his nightstand, next to his endless Maigret and the Japanese fisherman his colleagues gave him for retirement. The Tamara de Lempicka she painted used to be there too: it vanished that May day.

I was the one who found her, in the laundry room that opens on to the garage. It was once her parents' little eat-in kitchen after they moved here from Vergiano, before the rest of the house was built: a three-by-two-metre box with a sink, a table, a line for hanging laundry. She added a dresser for her brushes and tempera paints, her finished canvases, her succulents. And those inkwells from the late sixties. Why the late sixties in particular? They remind me of her days as a young teacher.

She was face down on the tiles, the iron near her left shoulder: we hadn't seen her for an hour. You could always hear Caterina: chatting with the neighbours, humming around the house or while watering plants, dragging her soles across the floor.

Her eyes were open. Left arm by her side, fist clenched. Right arm folded under her belly. On the ironing board: a button-down shirt.

He has left everything as it was: the temperas in the drawer, the box of inkwells, the canvases, the line with its clothes pegs, even though he now hangs clothes on the terrace to dry. He added the poster from the Baia Imperiale in Gabicce, the Grand Gala.

He helped me lift her, carry her into the garage. When we eased her back down, her pendant slid up towards her chin. Now it's in his study in the wooden box, the one with a third eye in gold leaf on the lid. I once asked her what that was and she said it was the penetrative part of each of us.

'So a dick,' I replied.

'Dummy.'

'What's yours?'

She said nothing.

'I'll tell you: patience.'

'Really?'

'Considering who you married.'

'Ah, true,' she said, laughing out loud.

Then he caught up with us, his steps hurried, as if late to the party.

'Welcome,' she said.

'Welcome to what?'
'To the third eye.'

And how he flaunted her, his beautiful Caterina. Having won her and kept her for himself, a medal to pin on his jacket.

As for her? She worried not about gaining or maintaining status, but about losing face: her shame regarding anything that might give rise to gossip (a faux pas, some excessive divergence from the norm) gave the lie to her alleged non-conformism. My dreadlocks at sixteen: you look revolting – have you seen yourself? Or my report cards, always in relation to others: and how were Walter's grades? Or my ad for sex lube: please don't mention that you're behind that one.

For both: a struggle between prizing the unconventional and dreading the scarlet letter.

At the bank, my credit limit increase is contingent on my putting up collateral. I was hoping my income documents and my history with the branch would be enough. They say it's determined by new parameters. I ask to speak to the manager – I've known him for years – and get an appointment for three days later.

At home I make notes on the two accounts: if they pay all the consultancy fees they owe me, I could get by for five more months, counting my Milan rent. Since my arrival in Rimini, he keeps trying to pay for all the groceries, but I've said I'll leave if we can't take turns.

'Stay.'
'If we split things.'

'What about your work?'

'I work fine here.'

He strokes his moustache the way he does when he's listening to a riveting story, or watching a war film and eating licorice. I don't know how that started, but that's how it is: war and licorice.

When we carried her to the garage, piss spread across her green dress. He took the sheet that was covering the bikes and put it over her.

'I'll call the ambulance.' He had pulled out his phone.

'I'll do it.'

He stood in the opening of the garage until they came with their sirens. I went out to meet them, and he went back in and got down on his knees to kiss her on the forehead.

Rimini, the new guy to fleece. Then: Rimini, the guy who never gives any trouble. Then: Rimini, who cleaned out two tables the other night. Then: Rimini, he looks like a kid but watch out.

On the day of my appointment with the bank manager I head out an hour early, on foot. The hills aren't close enough to cool off the coastal air, which is muggy and gritty with salt.

I walk along Marecchia Park, the river blathering, its reeds flattened by the recent storm. I take the road that ends at the Pari butcher shop and pause at the stop sign: here, at this tip of Ina Casa, is where the warm garbino swirls in from the sea. I spread my arms to let it fill my shirt, and I'm flying. In summer all roads lead to the beach and Rimini exists only at the seaside. Except for the voices: radios on porches, commotions in kitchens, the swishing of clothes on their lines. The chatter is handed off from house to house and trails me all the way to the church piazza. Don Paolo is waiting there for me in his red Lacoste, hands in his jean pockets, sweating heavily, and he falls in beside me. We walk as we did after she told him about my turn for the worse, and as we walked later, after she was gone: both of us grim, his carabiner chirping on his belt.

We head towards Via Marecchiese, silent this time too, until I tell him: at night Nando goes dancing.

'You sure?'

'I'm sure.'

He looks at me with relief, grips his carabiner and quickens his pace until we're in front of the bank.

He's the kind of priest for whom a nod is enough: he leaves me at the bank, doesn't insist on keeping watch. Be alone: he says that's the eleventh commandment. And the twelfth? Try to mind your own fucking business.

I enter and the manager takes me to his office and offers me coffee. We sit and sip, and he explains that the policy regarding lines of credit no longer allows for any exceptions, even for long-time customers. All he needs is a signature from my father – he saw him in the teller line a week ago. I make it clear that he is not to be involved in any way.

When I leave I consider asking Lele for help, or Walter, though Walter is already under pressure with his bar.

Without a line of credit: I'll have to leave Milan, move in with him, live here, on this street, its concrete and flowerbeds, these people, the faces of childhood and the noises of dawn, the town I'm always forgetting. Here, in Rimini. And I walk, undone, from the bank to the old town, nearly running as I reach Piazza Malatesta, lungs shrivelling, and stop: I sit, panting, tilting my face up toward Teatro Galli and its orange walls. Live here. My eyes burn but I keep staring at the Galli. For her, who would have loved to see it after its restoration, to hear it reopened by Riccardo Muti, whom she adored – and for him, who once got her tickets for Muti's Ravenna concert, trying to make amends.

'Amends for what?' I asked her.

'A blow-up,' she said. And she cried. They didn't go dancing that weekend. A month later we buried her.

'What happened with Mum? That blow-up you made up for with the Muti tickets.'

He pauses to gather his thoughts even though he remembers perfectly well, then he turns off the TV and fiddles with the lighter. 'A quarrel.'

'A quarrel.'

'Something like that.' He hides the lighter in his fist, looks around.

'She didn't cry about quarrels.'

He turns the television back on.

'She'd found out about the cat and about Pannella.'

'What cat?'

'The one in Montescudo that was wrecking the maple.'

'And?'

'I shot him.'

'Shot who?'

'The cat.'

'You're nuts.'

He changes the channel, turns it off again. 'Your mum found spots of blood near the outdoor table. She was already on edge because she'd just found out about Pannella.'

'Found out what about Pannella?'

'That I voted for him, twice.'

'You voted for the Radical Party?'

"94 and '96.'

'No way.'

He shakes his head. 'I was fed up.'

'And who'd she find out from?'

'From me. About the cat, too. I told her. It wasn't like we kept secrets.'

'So how'd you do it.'

'The rifle, a clean shot.'

They issue cheques every hundred and twenty days. They issue cheques every hundred and eighty days. But they aren't issuing cheques. Maybe he's right: I'm incapable of going after them. I shut myself in my room to call the companies that owe me. One is a communications agency that hired me to consult on the use of rental scooters by TikTok users. The other is a Crescenzago-based outfit that sells one hundred per cent sustainable costume jewellery.

I demand payment. The communications agency says again that it should go through in a matter of days. The Crescenzago business is certain that the bank transfer is already in process. What does 'already in process' mean? That it's under way. What does 'under way' mean? Today, or maybe tomorrow. Maybe? They assure me: tomorrow at the latest.

Hanging in the balance, as at the tables. That weariness: take home six hundred euros on Wednesday, lose eight on Friday, now some good luck, now a bad deck.

'You're scared to win, Sandro,' Bruni said early on, when I was still avoiding the big games.

It was Nando who introduced me to Bruni. August of 2003. At my cousin's wedding, in Longiano. Before the cake cutting he came up to me with this stocky, red-faced guy and introduced him as the son of his former colleague Maurizio, whom we'd gone on holiday with at Le Balze in 1979.

'You were both less than a year old, both always crying – we called you the Snivel Twins.'

And he left us on the terrace of the restaurant. Neither of us could remember Le Balze but Bruni was sure he'd seen me at Bagno 5, at the volleyball nets, the August after graduation when he was lifeguarding at the free beach.

'And after lifeguarding?'

'Architecture, but I'm about to quit. Meantime I'm working at the racetrack. Ever been?' And I noticed his mannerism of clicking the roof of his mouth.

'To the tracks? Once, when I was little.'

'The pay's good. Got me an Audi.'

We were quiet, a good kind of silence, and Bruni lit a cigarette and offered me one and I felt my shoulders loosen. We both took drags and he exhaled calm words with his smoke: 'You should come on Sunday, for the Palio – it's a fun time.'

After dinner he knocks on my door and asks if I took his chequered tie.

'I haven't taken one of your ties in twenty-five years.'

'Then where'd I put it.'

He leaves my room and rummages through drawers, one wardrobe, another wardrobe, the study, then goes downstairs and comes back up, then returns to me, purple.

'You sure you haven't seen it? The chequered one.'

'You'll find it tomorrow in the daylight.'

'I wanted to wear it tonight.'

'You're going out?'

He taps his heels. 'Coming?'

In ten minutes we're in jeans and button-down shirts in front of the mirror. No ties. I'm a head taller and he starts pulling down on my shoulder to lower me; I bend my knees to match his height. We look alike now: wild hair and bony faces, hollow eye sockets.

'Is that a paunch, Nando?'

He sucks it in and whistles a tune. Then he heads to the kitchen, yanks open the cupboard and takes out his heart pills and a sachet of pain relief powder, which he dissolves in water and drinks down. He's whistling again and is still at it as we're heading to the car. 'My wrecked back. I'm old.'

'I'll dance tonight.'

He stares at me to see if I'm telling the truth. And I am.

We get into the Renault 5 and he starts out slow to let the engine warm up. He drives gently out of Ina Casa, one hand on the wheel, then rolls through stop signs until we reach Piazza Tripoli. He backs into an angled space, his speciality. We hop out and head to the Atlantide. The neon is dazzling, its shimmer climbing to the roof. They're sparkling: the Atlantide and Rimini are sparkling.

The first time you get in by chance. An invitation, a lucky opportunity, and you're in. You're there at the table and you know how to handle yourself. The feeling: having learned a thing without anyone having taught you.

I start for the dance floor first. He passes me and does the honours, leading me to a spot in the fourth row and placing himself in front of me, so I can copy his steps. Next to me is a fiftyish woman in boots, high-waisted jeans and a white shirt. The song starts and my neighbour jumps to her left, and Nando does too. I keep behind him. And I see them and don't, those loose legs, the fringe of leather waistcoats, the rolled-up trouser legs, the faces distorted with excitement: they appear, vanish, and reemerge from the intermittent night of the Atlantide. Is that really my father, that man with the butterfly hips?

'Go, Sandrin!' he yells to me in mid-pirouette. And it's him, I know it's him, and both of us are cowboys.

Mark of a gambler: thinking will I or won't I throughout the day. At breakfast, at work, when I was with Giulia. Airy ideas of future games, working out the maths to be able to play. Thinking will I or won't I, itself a kind of game.

I do five songs and am about to leave it at that but my dance neighbour urges me to stay. Her name is Lucia and she's from Verucchio, comes here once a week by herself.

After the second song she's been shouting out my steps in advance.

'Whoa,' I yell. 'I'm worn out.'

'Three months to get used to the pace,' she yells back.

He laughs, stays.

I walk to the bar in my John Wayne hat, order an Americano cocktail and take a seat near the dance floor. He's taken my spot, in Lucia's line.

The music starts up again and they move in unison. What would he be like with another woman. What's he like now, without her. And I'm looking at him and Nando is looking back at me, and I feel a shyness I felt as a child.

When they were about to bury her he disappeared. At the cemetery were former pupils from Caterina's teaching days, all grown up, along with friends old and new, not many wearing black. And lots of tulips. She liked those.

Don Paolo and I found him smoking behind the main chapel. He finished his cigarette, and when we returned together they were ready to lower her with the ropes.

He went over, craned his neck, and asked whether it would be sealed with mortar or inset.

He dances two more songs and takes his leave from the music with a half bow. Then we leave the Atlantide.

It's dark, but it's the darkness of Marina Centro, which is like daylight. Sweaty, we hurry to the Renault 5. I insist on driving; he hesitates but agrees.

We get in the car and catch our breath. I lean my seat back a little and he leans his back too. He's looking out his window and massaging his kidney area, the sky outside is clear, the Tripoli sign is gleaming on the pavement. I'm about to start the car but he reaches for my elbow. Holds it there, his grip gentle, his fingers cold. Then lets go and adjusts the rearview for me. 'I haven't wanted it since your mother,' he says, buckling his seatbelt.

I buckle up too.

'Have you wanted it since Giulia?'

I start the engine. 'Lele thinks I should marry this Bibi.'

'What's she like?'

'I haven't wanted it either.'

Being ready whenever the possibility of a game arose. Getting the call. Or making the call. The mad rush to gather the cash to go and knock on the door.

We keep the seats tilted back the whole way, and when we reach Ina Casa we slow down. Seen from here Largo Bordoni is an amphitheatre, with its squat blocks of apartments and their lit windows acting as audience for the square. I ask if he'll join me for a cream puff at Bar Zeta.

We go. He doesn't order one and then does. He takes two bites and leaves the rest for me. He has a powdered-sugar moustache, and I snap a picture of him with my phone and send it to him without saying anything. He sees it as we're parking back at the house.

'Look at that face. I'm old,' he says.

'Oh stop it.'

He's getting ready to light a cigarette. 'I don't have long, Sandrin.'

'Stop it.'

'That's what they say down at the hospital.'

October, November

The Pasadèl: his Railway Social friends stuck him with that Romagnolo nickname in the mid-nineties, after seeing him dance at the Festa de l'Unità. In standard Italian, the Passatello: a delicate pasta, simple ingredients, substantial returns. Nando Pagliarani, the Pasadèl.

'You mind them calling you that?'

'Passatelli make a good soup.' I help him pull himself up. He dresses himself, goes into the bathroom. I hear him shake the aftershave bottle and give it a squirt, then he comes back out and says he feels like taking a walk in the garden. First we have tea and dry biscuits, and he nibbles. Then he walks slowly ahead of me down the front steps and stops in front of the vegetable plot.

'What a shame, Sandro.'

'I'll look after it.'

'You don't enjoy it.'

'You don't know that.'

'C'mon.'

'I'll add earthworms to the strawberries, ash to the tomatoes with a powder duster for the spider mites. Plant during a waxing moon.'

He's not convinced. He wants his fisherman's cap, I fetch it from the garage and he tugs it on and his face disappears beneath the brim. We set up two folding chairs at the edge of the garden – his is the one with navy and white stripes. He sits down.

'Show me.'

'Now?'

'Sure.'

To him, how you hold a spade is as important as how you hold a tennis racket. His taunting chant when we used to go to the Italian Open: see Rafa gripping semi-western, see Roger gripping any old way.

'Go on, show me.'

I push up my sweater sleeves and grab the spade. I get into position beside a row of squash.

'Fingers a little higher, get 'em up.'

I get them up.

'There, good job.'

'Here.'

'Imagine what fine tomatoes will come of this.'

His strong legs: six times out of ten he can stand by himself. The other night with Prince on the turntable he shook his feet. Today he accepts the stronger anti-inflammatory his oncologist suggested.

'Turns out she's not such a Medusa, this doctor of mine.'

'Meanest doctor in Italy.'

'I never told you...' He's tired, his voice is in his nose. 'It was a Tuesday. I walked into her office and she didn't even offer me a seat. She let me have it right away, the bad news. That that's what was causing the bloated belly and the back pain and the white shit. That it had spread. We were both stock still, and she really looked like some

Medusa. But she also had this calm, as if she were saying The weather's bad today or We'll need some ground beef for the meatballs. A lovely calm.'

'What's that even mean.'

'And I walked out of the hospital still feeling that lovely calm. I went to the covered market and bought some anchovies.' He runs a hand over his face and smiles, as if appreciating a simple story. 'And after that I made the piada, picked some endive and onions, cleaned the anchovies and put them in the pan.'

'Was it good?'

'Obviously it was good.'

'And then?'

'Then I called you and you were at the supermarket buying frozen stuff.'

We've moved our card games to the afternoon. It's twenty-one to seventeen in his favour. We're playing rummy in bed, him leaning against the headboard and me sitting diagonally. Between games we smooth out the blanket so the cards don't get tilted up – tilted cards drive us both crazy.

I win the first. I win the second, too, and his head flops back on his pillow in annoyance. He closes his eyes, starting to fall asleep. He opens them wide. 'The troubles steer clear of Rimini, eh?'

'What troubles.'

'Your troubles.'

'There's no trouble.'

He picks up the deck, closes his eyes again, and shuffles.

Two months ago eight thousand euros showed up in my account. I got a notification on my phone, checked and saw that it was him. I found him watching a replay of the Nadal–Coria match from the 2005 Italian Open.

'What's the deal,' I said, showing him the transfer notification.

'The interest.'

'What interest?'

'The downstairs renovation.'

'Oh, that five thousand you paid me back after three weeks. For a house you renovated for me?'

'Take Bibi down there.'

'You want to humiliate me.'

He didn't take his eyes off Nadal.

'You want to humiliate me.'

'Look at the forehand Rafa had already when he was twenty.'

I'd accepted Bruni's invitation to the racetrack. He met me at the entrance, led me to the monitors. From there you could see the track and the terrace with the outdoor tables. His job was to supervise the events and the preparation of the horses. He pointed out the name of a trotter on the left monitor, Sunrise92.

'Spotlight on Sunrise today, Sandro.'

'He's strong?'

'On paper. The smart money's on the middling favourites or long shots,' and he lowered his finger to the middle of the monitor: 'Emmet88.'

'What smart money?'

'Bets.'

'Bets.'

'Bets.'

I was standing close to the monitor. 'Let me know if he wins.'

'You're not staying?'

I had to see my professor about my thesis, so I was leaving for Bologna.

'Well, put down a little something, at least.'

'Where?'

'I have a friend. How does five euros on our Emmet sound? He's at six to one, so you'd take home a nice chunk.'

'And if he doesn't win.'

'You're out five and that's it.'

Some mornings he asks me to open the windows even though it's cool out. October and November are his months. Because of the persimmons. As a child he would climb the tree and pick one and eat it under the walnut tree, with Mascarin barking at him.

'Persimmons in November, jujubes in August,' he mumbles as I cut his hair. I'm trimming the back of his neck, which isn't quite right, using my hand as a pincer to block it. He's picking at the spot below his collar bone where they implanted the chemo port.

'Would you have done that last round of treatment?' He asks with a tilt of his head. 'It would buy you three extra months.'

I turn off the clippers. 'What would you do with three more months and a million euros?'

He grins. 'A nitwit, you are.'

The others drop in to see him: Lele, Walter, Don Paolo. They wave from the bottom of the stairs and go, or come up if he's not too tired, or say hi from the street if we're out in the garden chairs. One afternoon they all happened by at the same time and had coffee in Nando's room. And seeing us there – him, me, them, all men – it occurred to me that we lost the thread of our lives as soon as the women left.

Today only Lele comes. He lingers for a long time: they talk about films. Pro-Troisi, anti-Troisi: for Lele he was the heir of De Filippo; Nando doesn't even like *Il postino*.

Apropos of nothing he declares: 'Gaetano Scirea.'

He informs me that he's arranged the will with the notary Lorenzi, a formality. And that he wants to go over some details with me about the boiler, maintenance, stuff I'll need to know to keep things running. Though in any case the 'Due dates' folder in his study covers all of that.

'Go on, get some rest.'

'So you don't want to know about the will?'

I don't.

'Good thing Bar America's not still around. Or I'd leave you in debt.'

'You'd leave me a job.'

He's not sure whether to laugh. 'What about the university?'

'Next term.'

'Salary?'

'Fifteen before taxes.'

'Fifteen before taxes,' he says, doing the maths in his head, dividing the total by the number of months. 'What about Nike?'

'You liked that idea, eh?'

'It was nice.'

'They haven't replied yet.'

'Not replying, not paying you. What a shitty time.'

'And you worrying about my vice.'

'The pocket change from the will,' he says, looking out through the French doors. 'As far as I'm concerned you can blow it all.'

The five euros I gave to Bruni, for Emmet88. My hand opening my wallet like an accordion, extracting the note, handing it over: thinking I'll never see that again. But feeling in my heart that it would come back, multiplied.

He has a hard time eating. Cream cheese on a crust of almond cake, half a chicken cutlet, some crackers.

'Whatcha make yourself today?' he asks.

'Pasta.'

'Pasta how?'

'With pesto.'

'Light the stove with a match?'

'A lighter.'

'Cooks better with a match.'

'Rubbish.'

'Sheesh, that head of yours. Poor Bibi.'

'She doesn't cook either.'

'How do you manage?'

'We go to a restaurant.'
'Yeah, Café Disgraceful.'

And that thought, right after giving Bruni the five euros for the bet: to double the stakes. And doing it: reopening my wallet and giving him a ten instead.

They always cooked together, him at the stove and her back and forth between fridge and sink. They'd meet over the counter, by the coffee maker: chopping, deboning, peeling, seasoning.

She did the fish, on Fridays. He always did the meat, which in winter in Romagna we eat almost every day. In hot weather on the other hand, pasta at lunch and veggies with skewers of calamari for dinner. The piada was her domain: she kneaded the dough and rolled the flatbread out herself, without lard and with oil from Montescudo. He had nothing to do with that.

When he's not having respiratory crises or hip pain, the palliative care people come once a week to check in and adjust dosages. He's become stubborn and no longer wants to use the morphine pump. He'll take it as needed. He doesn't want the anti-bedsore pad, doesn't want the bed rails.

This time it's two nurses and they arrive after I've been calling urgently for an hour: his lymph nodes are causing back pain. He's suffering without complaint, eyes glassy, legs wooden. Last night we moved pillows around under his body until we found a good position.

'Ah, the pillows,' he said as the sun was coming up. 'The pillows and that time you died.'

That time I died there were seven of us at Mulazzani's farm on the east side of Covignano. Spring equinox of my final year in school. I was supposed to go into the sow pen with two other guys and pick up one of the newborns. Pick it up, take it out of the pen and pass it around, each of us asking the Virgin for blessings. Once upon a time we would have sacrificed it, but time has softened us.

I went into the pen and took one of the little ones but slipped, and the sow charged me. They barely pulled me out in time – I lost consciousness and was in intensive care for a while. I came home a month later to find him in the bedroom with all these pillows – how do you want them, I can put them here, I can put them under you, next to you – until I found relief.

'What if I really had died, Nando?'

He shows me the back of his hand: his dying man's way of saying fuck off.

Then it starts: 'What are we doing?'

It's a refrain some days, it starts slowly and picks up speed: What are we doing? What are we doing?

The first few times I asked him in what sense, and he just repeated: What are we doing?

It's one of those questions that betrays an awareness of the end: that's what the hospital psychologist says. He keeps on asking for an hour or two, sometimes in a whisper, flaring his nostrils and sucking in his cheeks. He dozes off. As soon as he wakes up again, the question takes physical form: he squeezes the sheets, sits up and then lies back down.

It starts again.

'What are we doing, Sandrin?'

I caress his hands. 'What do you want to do?'

'Damn it all,' he hisses between his teeth.

An imprecation I used to hear as a child when the numbers didn't add up or when he was hacking at a rogue root in the garden.

I stopped gambling for eleven months. Then I started again one Friday in April. It was morning and Giulia had left for work. She still wore her hair in a bob – or maybe not: gambling always muddled my image of her.

I notified my agency that I wouldn't be coming into the office, got dressed and went out. I went to Piazzale Loreto and withdrew two hundred and fifty with my debit card, another two fifty with a credit card. I had sorted the notes by denomination even before calling to see if I could find a sit-and-go game.

Sit-and-go games: people without references, travellers, unpredictable regarding debts. Novices to fleece and hidden alliances. Bad beats and filthy bluffs.

I got out my phone and called. They took their time getting back to me but twenty minutes later I was offered a seat at a game in the Solari district, starting two hours from then. Two hundred buy-in, no limit.

I went home and got our chequebook and the four hundred in cash we kept for emergencies.

The Solari game was in an apartment on Via Montevideo, in a building with majolica tiles on the main balcony, decorations on the eaves and red geraniums. Milan, where the destiny of the individual gets muddled by the haste of others.

I waited on a park bench, next to a woman with a terrier on her lap, and watched the entryway from afar. The first player showed up early, as did the second. Restlessness unites us: we mill around, we stand still, tormenting the pavements with our soles; we rummage through our pockets and pull out our fists, then pocket them again; we smoke and chew American gum.

I waited ten minutes before going in. I went up, greeted the others, holding on to my jacket until I got my bearings. I checked out the table and the seats, confirmed that the deck was new and sealed. I went over to the bar and wet my lips with an amaro. When the fourth player arrived, I bought chips, small and medium denominations.

I took a seat, stretching my legs to see how much space I'd have. A foreigner, Russian maybe, sat next to me, his eyebrows drowning his eyes. He began talking to himself: harsh tones, guttural sounds, a habit of thrusting out and retracting his chin.

Then cards were dealt. The Russian talked to himself, fell silent, smoked. I lost three hundred and sixty: I had five forty left in my pocket, plus the chequebook with the three thousand in our joint account.

Then the second hand: the cards were shuffled, I was dealt a pair of sevens, the Russian exchanged three cards, we went around, the pot grew. At my twelve o'clock a Venetian with a goatee and a velvet jacket, at my three o'clock a woman in her thirties with tiny sparkly earrings. I imagined winning them for Giulia – personal effects are permissible commodities.

I raised and they called, we exchanged cards and I bet, they raised and I reraised in turn, then folded. The

Russian won fourteen hundred, the Venetian had limited the damage.

We played a third hand that was taken by a chameleon in his mid-forties, silent, titanium-rimmed glasses. Chameleons: players who sit quietly to get a feel for the table, waiting for the moment to strike.

We took a break before the last hand. I got up, everyone did, and went over to the window. I always sought out windows during breaks. This one overlooked the park: the woman with the terrier on her lap was gone, the bench now empty. At the table the remains of cigarettes rose from the ashtrays. I stood there at the window; the Russian was buying more chips, the Venetian was sitting on a sofa. The chameleon was loitering around the bar, the woman was leaning against a wall and twirling her watch around her wrist. I had two hundred and change in chips, enough to play and leave my net intact. Leaving a net: limiting how much you risk, absorbing manageable damage.

I took out my chequebook and wrote a cheque for another eighteen hundred.

He wails and wails: in the evening, just before midnight or right after. He's lamenting the end of the day. His howls trail off into gurgles.

The hours that follow are uncertain. He'll sleep, or read a page of something, or watch some TV, or ask about Bibi.

Tonight he wants the photo album. He flips through the pages, tells how his mother had a white filly and a buggy for her Sunday rounds in San Zaccaria. 'I'd pay a hundred grand to go back there,' he says, coughing.

'Did she drive the horse herself?'

'I'll sell this place and use a hundred grand to go back to one of those Sundays, to that buggy with the filly.'

'A hundred grand's not enough.'

'And you?'

'Me what?'

'A memory, and how much you'd pay.'

I laugh. 'These fucked-up games of ours.'

'Your games sure but not mine.'

I lie back on the bed and think, though I already have the answer: 'I'm with Caterina in the kitchen, sitting on the counter, a couple of days before Christmas. I'm little and those biscuits with coloured sugar are baking in the oven, and she whispers: tomorrow's Christmas Eve, Muccio.'

'Nice.'

'Thinking about that makes me happy.'

'How much would you pay?'

'Fifty grand.'

'And what would you pay a hundred for? Bibi?'

'You're obsessed, you are.'

'Your mother would've liked her.'

'You barely even know her.'

'Like that other one, Giulia.'

'What does she have to do with this?'

'Your mother was convinced you never brought her around because you knew you'd've gambled her away too.'

'But I did bring her.'

'Three times.'

'And so?'

'So cards also take away your feelings for women.'

I adjust my pillow. 'Anyway: fifty thousand for Bibi.'

'Fifty thousand for a three-month crush?'

'She's pretty.'

'How pretty?'

I stretch. 'It's going well.'

'In that case a hundred for Bibi. And another hundred for what?'

'Sheesh, gimme a break, Nando.'

'C'mon,' he growls. 'C'mon.'

I look up at the ceiling. 'That night at the Notte Rosa, dealt three of a kind.'

'Ah.'

'Yeah.'

'And how much did you win?'

'Not that much. But being dealt three of a kind...'

'Ever been dealt four of a kind?'

'Uh, no.'

'No? One two three four – you'd've liked that.'

'Sure.'

'Ever happen to anyone you know?'

I nod. 'Guy from Buccinasco.'

'And how much did he win?'

'Can't remember.'

'Was he happy?'

'It's not like we're ever happy, us.'

'Us?'

'You should've been a border control interrogator down at the Port Authority.'

'But what are your kind like, c'mon.'

And I feel like saying: we're in the thick of life.

But he's distracted, puts a hand over his mouth and quickly takes it off. 'Four nice cards like that. Add a nice pool to that ruin of a house.'

71

'What does your ruin have to do with this?'

'It's my dream hand.'

'In that case a penthouse in Buenos Aires.'

He tilts up his nose. 'Not London?'

'I dream about Buenos Aires too.'

'And strigoli omelettes.'

'And tits.'

'And locomotives that used to whistle in the station as we listened from the garage. And Tina Turner. And that filly with the buggy.'

'And cards.'

He lowers his head. 'Ugh, I knew it.'

'If you knew then why'd you ask? I've got cards and you've got the filly.'

'We'd take her out early on Sunday afternoons.'

I pull myself up and help him find a different position.

He holds on tight. 'And some Sundays it was Dad who took the reins.'

Later Don Paolo stops by for the second time and rings the doorbell. Nando leaves him hanging again but after three minutes looks out the window and finds him still there.

'Tell him to come up.'

I offer Paolo coffee but he declines, unclipping his carabiner, leaving his keys on the table with his jacket.

In the bedroom, he makes his way around the bed to sit on Nando's side.

I take refuge in the living room, the kitchen, the living room again, then I go down to the courtyard, glancing up at their room.

They spend an hour together. When they're done Paolo puts his carabiner and jacket back on, and I rejoin him.

'You know what Andreotti once said to me? He said: in the end it's always the romantics who have the most faith.'

'Nando, a romantic?'

'Despite being a card-carrying communist for nine years.'

When I go back up the TV's on, he's channel surfing, and his side is hurting. He accepts the morphine and stares at me. 'I asked Paolo if it's better to be a believer or to be believable.'

I put a blanket on him. 'Neither one.'

'He's sure I'll meet her. Your mum, I mean.'

He wants to go and find her, he says casually as he gets up to make his way to the bathroom.

'Need to shave first, though.'

I get his shaving kit ready and bring him the chair. He sits and studies himself in the mirror.

Meanwhile I go to my room to get my laundry basket: one pair of trousers and a denim shirt are the only clean things I have left. Plus some old stuff in the wardrobe: a tracksuit, a corduroy blazer, a tattered sweatshirt. I tell him I'm going back to Milan to get some more clothes and to stop by the university. I look for his box of medical files to take to the Milan hospitals – the IEO, Niguarda. I can't find them.

'Just go to Milan already,' he says.

'But where'd you put them?'

'Forget those.'

'The hell I will.'

'Forget those,' he repeats, voice thin. 'The Adriatic is definitely not in Milan.'

I go back to the bathroom. He's tilting his face towards the light, tracing the outline of his nose with his index finger. 'I'm grey. Let's stay at home.'

We rarely played in the same house twice. The few that recurred were safe, made available by the organisation on a rotating basis or by estate agents who hadn't been able to rent them and so hired them out for brief periods – half a day, six hours, a full day. Cash in hand, plus cleaning fees. Via Vitruvio, Via Fiamma, Corso Vercelli – preferably outside Milan's second circle. The places were almost always empty except for the table and chairs and a sofa. Once for five months we used a vacant apartment on Via Bazzini: cherry panelling, a bathtub with dog-paw feet, diamond-pattern wallpaper, jelly sweets in a silver tureen.

We made no loud noises, left no traces, and came and went one at a time.

'You gambled because that's what you're like, Sandrin.'

'Like what?'

'Like that, a little here, a little there.'

'I gambled because I like it and that's it.'

'What does that mean? I like playing cards too but I don't put my shekels there.'

'Because you never had the chance.'

'Not true. In Milano Marittima, those guys would hang out at the depot and millions would change hands.'

'And you weren't interested?'

'I had girls.'

He mostly wants to be alone and not talk to anyone. But it depends on the day: if he's feeling good he'll answer calls. He's often typing on his phone. Occasionally he'll trumpet the arrival of some distant relative or old colleague. Today he announces: a friend from Cervia is coming.

'Wait, you have friends?'

He once admitted that he'd lost his friends after getting married. What remained was a tennis game with some guys from the railway and evenings with the husbands of her friends. He'd be getting along, holding court, and then one day: I'm not sure about so-and-so. Why not? Gut feeling. So-and-so doesn't do it for me anymore. How come? Gut feeling. Does so-and-so seem fake to you? Why do you say that? Gut feeling. And a gut feeling that they were all in love with his Caterina.

The friend from Cervia really does come. He doesn't take off his jacket. He has girlish eyebrows and an obscure way of speaking. He calls Nando by name: Ferdinando. At one point I hear them snickering – the mirth of their youth?

I was on the train to Bologna when my mobile lit up with a Rimini area code. I answered. A voice told me I'd won sixty.

'Excuse me?'

'Sixty euros, my friend.'

'What?'

'Emmet88.'

'Bruni, is that you?'

'You did well to bet ten instead of five.'

'Emmet won?'

'You've got the gift, Sandro.'

His rust-orange elbow-patch sweater that smells like after-shave: he eyes me in it like he used to when I swiped stuff from him as a kid.

'And straighten up, you look like a hunchback.'

I straighten up. I stand in front of him running a hand over my chest, stomach, sides, arms, to smooth the wool. 'Is it too tight?'

'Looks good on you.' He signals for me to come closer. He reaches out and smooths the lower back.

'Caterina once soaked it for a day and couldn't get my smell out.'

He closes his eyes.

'Hello, Sandro? I've got another horse for you. Hot tip.'

'Bruni, hi. I'm in Bologna, can I call you back?'

'The favourite's in a bad way but nobody knows. I've got a lightning bolt from north of the Alps that'll burn him.'

'I'm spending the sixty I won at the Diana. Know it? The tortellini in brodo is heavenly.'

'Invest twenty on this lightning bolt. It's a hot tip.'

'I don't know, Bruni.'

'With your gift that's a shame.'

'Twenty?'

'Twenty.'

He always falls asleep around eight in the evening but his sleep is sporadic: we keep the doors open so if he needs me I can hear him. He asks to go to the bathroom, or to change positions, or once last month to go out on the terrace for the first briskness in the air.

This time he sleeps straight through and I do as well. I wake at dawn and rush in to him: he's awake and quiet with the air of someone who has been keeping watch over the night.

'Two things, Sandro.'

'Tell me.'

'We need some help, that nurse from Via Dario Campana, 'cause you're knackered.'

'I'm not tired.'

He takes a breath: 'And the other thing is I wanna take your mum some flowers.'

'I'll take them for you.'

'I'm comin'.'

'Today?'

'Can't do tomorrow.'

We're in no rush: we put on our tracksuits, one piece at a time. We help each other down the stairs, climb into the car. He's glad we're taking the Renault 5. I've tilted his seat back, he wedges a pillow against the door, and when we start out and jolt on to the road, he gives me the thumbs up. After I pick up speed the Renault 5 wobbles less. In the end he decided against bringing flowers.

It takes us twenty minutes, him criticising me for cutting the curves, and when we arrive he immediately notices Lele waiting for us in the open area in front of the cemetery. He's leaning against his Alfa MiTo.

'You inconvenienced him.'

'A helping hand.'

Lele opens his door, catches the pillow before it falls. We help Nando out and make our way, arms linked, to the columbarium hill. We climb the steps with him swaying between us.

'Sorry, guys.'

'For what,' Lele says, then leaves us to ourselves.

I take him to her, help him sit on the bench, then step back. He rests his chin on his right hand and his elbow on the armrest, looking at her.

When we get home he's worn out. Still, he notices that I left the light on in the bathroom.

'I'll turn it off later.'

'Always later, with you.'

I don't have time to get him ready for bed. He collapses. His eyes are half-closed, his voice a dirge. I lay him down as best I can and raise the blinds, letting the light of early evening in.

I go out of the room and feel like closing the door but leave it ajar. I take a shower. I heat up a piada, find some prosciutto and some stracchino. I chew and gulp it down. Outside: the Sabatini family lighting their grill, a plume of smoke coiling up, the bent streetlight. A succulent on the sill, which we use as a shelf. The old coffee grinder, sitting pretty.

'How long does he have?'

'Months, maybe three.' His oncologist kept me standing too. 'As long as his pancreas has.'

'He never told me.'

She went around her desk to sit, offered me a chair. I stood there: a lemon-yellow wall, at one end a photo of a child dressed as a fencer. But no lovely calm.

Three months. Today makes four. Some evenings he tells me about the Sabatinis' Christmas lights: if they put them up early again as usual, that will make five months.

I won with Emmet88, I won with the hot tip about the lightning bolt from north of the Alps. Back at the racetrack, I watched the monitors with Bruni, we wandered around, he showed me the stables. This time the idea was a French trotter. If I bet ten, I could win thirty-five euros. There was also a trotter, thought to be washed-up, from an Italian team: ten would pay one twenty.

We'd stopped at a stall where they were massaging the rump of an Orlov.

'I'm betting both. French and Italian.'

Bruni stared at me. He clicked the roof of his mouth.

'You like the races, you do.'

'If I had to pick, I'd take cards.'

'Yeah?'

'As a kid I played with my grandfather and always won.'

Patrizia? Patrizia from Sardinia. With me that's how he always referred to her. Patrizia Long-Shower is what I called her in my head. I haven't seen her since the funeral – a few words on the landline when I was visiting Rimini, a card.

She arrives after lunch with her cloak and a gift, fear in her eyes. She hugs me – the smell of juniper, the swimsuit lowered under the stream of water. Nostrils tingling. The summer of 1998.

I tell her he's napping, and she accepts coffee. It's her: the flicker across her face, top pulled down off her chest. Lifting her lowered head.

We talk about nothing: the dog with its hip problems, the move to Rimini from Morciano, October that feels like September. Then she sees the recipe book: 'Caterina's ragú.'

'With that brazen ingredient.'

'Ground pancetta.'

I sip my coffee.

She sips too. 'In the end your mum had a good time.' She wipes her mouth with a paper towel and her eyes lose their fear. He calls to her from his room.

I was sitting at a table in the Brera district with half of what Giulia and I had saved in our 'future account'. That's the name she gave it, the day after we went to the bank to open it. I withdrew the money at a branch office on the eve of the Feast of Sant'Ambrogio.

The game was on the third floor of a low building behind San Simpliciano. The building was the colour of whitewash: old Milan with widows in the windows.

I played loose because there were no fish, just folks from the good circle – a get-together, among intimates. Intimates of what?

I got away with it for the first two hands: won twelve hundred with two pair and folded a pair of sevens without much bleeding. Then the pots grew. Soon I was down eighteen hundred, and by the end I'd lost everything and written an IOU for three hundred.

He falls asleep before I have a chance to clear off the bed: the Bologna newspaper, his water bottle, cigarettes and an ashtray, the Celentano record that Patrizia from

Sardinia has given him. They were in there talking for forty minutes.

I doze off in my room and am awakened by his foot tapping against his bed. He leaves it dangling and his heel has started up, as it does each night.

Instead of going back to sleep I sit up and turn on the light. I reach towards the nightstand and leave my hand there, open, over the files for a rhubarb aperitivo commercial, a box of biscuits, a bottle of chinotto. On my phone, a message from Bibi: she'd rather go out with the two of us than with Lele and the others. She suggests Saturday. I don't know how to manage that with Nando.

The heel stops tapping and he calls me.

I go in. His head is raised and with one hand he lifts the sheet, points to his pyjamas. 'Disgusting,' he whispers.

'Now we'll clean up.'

In the bathroom he undresses himself; I help with the trousers. I ask him to sit in the shower cubicle; he seems distressed and avoids the plastic stool.

'I'll stand.'

'Just sit.'

'We gotta put the whatsit on, Sandrin. I'm pissing myself.'

'We said no nappies, didn't we? Just sit.'

Stubborn, he doesn't sit. I give him the body wash and wait as the water runs. He's always aware of my squeamishness. I show no reaction, yet he stares at me: he knows my scream is his. His body naked, empty, his veins bulging, his belly swollen above his pubic area: this knobby cock that has survived disease.

Our first trip to Rome for tennis was an early present for his sixty-sixth birthday. I'd wrapped the tickets, and when he opened them he didn't understand at first.

'The final,' she explained on my behalf.

'The final,' he repeated, eyeing them more closely. He stored them in the trumeau cabinet in the living room, waiting for May. Sometimes he'd check on them, she told me, and when the day came we travelled by train, he from Rimini and I from Milan. We arranged to meet in Bologna to finish the journey together.

When we reached Rome, he tried to carry my suitcase into the metro and then from the metro to Via dei Gracchi, where I had booked our hotel. At the front desk I said I had reserved a twin room, and he stood expressionless, ID in hand, as he learned he would be sharing a room with his son.

I left him the bed by the window, which he sat on to test. He took over the bathroom: his aftershave, toothbrush and toothpaste on the sink. He unpacked, put his clothes on hangers, slid the wheeled cabin bag into the wardrobe, and turned to me. 'Keep it tidy, Sandro.'

'Don't start.'

We had dinner in a little restaurant next door, carbonara and wine from the Roman Hills, followed by chicory sautéed with chillies. We barely spoke until we were done and strolling through Piazza del Popolo, the tang of anticipation in the air: tomorrow, the match. And the later it got, the shyer I began to feel, going back to the hotel, up the stairs, into our room, and his turn in the bathroom, and my turn in the bathroom, and then finding ourselves in our underpants and T-shirts on the two beds half a metre apart.

It was then that we called Caterina: Yes everything's fine even if Nando's hogging the wardrobe, Hey gimme the phone you nitwit. Afterwards he put on his glasses to study the map of Rome and I stayed on my phone, then we turned off the bedside lamps and said goodnight as a streetlight from Via dei Gracchi filtered through the slats of the blinds, outlining his form, first on his side, then on his back, chest rising and falling until the snoring began.

In the morning – as in Val di Fassa, or Sardinia, or that time in London – he had a fearful but intrepid air about him. In his backpack, two hats and a K-Way rain jacket and a spare T-shirt; in his trouser pocket, his heart pills. We tightened when we reached the Foro Italico, but I'm not sure how to explain what I mean by *tight*: shoulder to shoulder, each on alert during minimal separations, with me moderating his urgency and him moderating my calm.

We caught sight of centre court, but as we approached he realised with a gasp that the finalists were warming up on nearby courts. He made his way over, chin high, legs quick to see if we could squeeze in. When we found a seat in front of Nadal, who was swatting forehands, he sat there a minute, backpack on his lap, saying Would ya look at that, and then handed me my hat and put his on.

At two o'clock sharp we were in our seats at centre court. The heat of early afternoon had alarmed him, so he sought out higher ground, near the top of the stadium. We watched the match on the edges of our seats, him huffing about Nadal's missed shots but also cheering for Federer as soon as he realised he was having back trouble. And already that urgency again: the urgency to get home to tell her all about it.

'Pissed myself like a kid.'

I help him out of the shower. He wants to sit in front of the mirror. Before he does he gives his left foot a little shake, making it dance.

'Hey hey the Pasadèl.'

'I don't have it anymore.'

'The Scirea Hop.'

'What a night that was – the Grand Gala with your mum, at the Baia Imperiale in Gabicce.'

I dry his back and shoulders, his neck, down to his lower back and up again as he dabs his ribs and belly with another towel. This time he hasn't asked for music.

He folds the towel over his legs, making a rectangle. 'You know what, Sandro? I'll use the million from our game to go up to Switzerland and call it a day.'

'That's a new one.'

'I'm serious.'

'It doesn't cost a million to croak legally.' I take the hair-dryer and dry the back of his head. 'I wish I had hair like this at my age.'

'And they tried to make it fall out,' he rasps. 'Just fold it over to the right there.'

Instead I tousle it, Volonté-style.

The Baia Imperiale, up in Gabicce. The Grand Gala with her. The Pasadèl and his invention, the Scirea Hop.

I look for the photos and can't find them. I ask where he put them. There weren't any, Sandrin. But I've seen them.

84

They never existed: your mum told the story of the Gala so often that we ended up with photos in our heads.

I go back to the study, rummage through the albums – nothing.

The rotation of an ankle, the twist of a hip: that was her workout. She'd put her legs in the air and draw circles with her feet, clockwise and counterclockwise, stretching the ligaments, getting the muscles warm. For the boogie-woogie, for the shag. Moving before the music moved her.

And him: those pelvic gyrations with an invisible hula-hoop, freeing up the femur, lining up the bones. All to spin Caterina from one side to the other: the grip on her hand, the yo-yo extension.

On the night of Ferragosto, they phoned my parents' house to tell them that because their son wasn't paying his gambling debts, they would take it out on his family.

He called me the next day in Milan as if nothing were wrong. How are you, What's up. Then she called and told me everything. She added, 'Your dad wept.'

'But tell me: what did the voice on the phone sound like?'

'Won't you ever stop with this business?'

'What was the voice like?'

'Polite. A man's voice.'

'Polite and?'

'If you don't pay we'll all end up badly.'

'C'mon.'

'How much do you owe them?'

'Eight hundred thousand.'

'Oh my God.'

'Just imagine.'

'Sandro, be serious.'

'I am serious.'

'I'll give it to you if you quit this business. Tell me how much money you owe.'

'What money.'

'Tell me the truth.'

'Stop it.'

'I'll give it to you.'

'I said stop it!'

'You stop!' And she wept too. 'My son's an addict.'

Before I fall asleep, I hear a thud from his room. I run. He's clinging to the curtain. Standing on one leg, the other is drawn up.

I put an arm under his.

He squirms, tries to right himself, the curtain tears away, and he falls.

I bend down to pick him up.

He writhes on the ground: a cockroach on its back. He grabs the other curtain and tries to pull himself up. It tears away too.

'The fuck are you doing,' I say, grappling with him, trying to lift him up.

He pushes me away.

I grab him again and pull him up, he thrashes, I drag him to the bed. His ribs are sharp. I rest half his backside on the mattress, he shoves my hands away, hits my arm, shoves me, hits me.

'Ow!' I shout.

He hits me again.

'Ow!'

I block him but he brings a hand back to slap me.

I pull myself up, lose my balance, and slam into the night-stand. I'm wedged against the wall and the Japanese fisherman figurine, regaining my balance. 'The fuck are you doing.'

'Going, to the kitchen.'

'Where the fuck are you going.' I hurl the fisherman to the floor. The shards ring and he cranes his neck to see if it has really happened, and as soon as he sees, he slumps. Then he turns his eyes to the door and watches me leave.

After he told me about his diagnosis, on cowboy night, he sat down on his front steps. He put his hands in his pockets and sat there, legs stretched out and shirt collar askew.

'It's nice hanging out together, Sandrin.'

I leave him among the fisherman shards. I get in my car and drive around, have a beer at Bar Sergio, then another, snack on crisps and almond brittle. They've replaced the slot machine with electronic darts. I play a game: of my five throws, three land within a centimetre of the bezel. One of the old guys watches and then goes back to reading his paper.

When I return, the light's on in his room. I go up and look in on him: he's sitting on the floor, leaning back against the bed. He's trying to gather up the pieces of the fisherman.

'Throw it away,' he mumbles. 'Throw everything away.'

I go over, and this time he lets me help him. I pull him up, put him to bed.

'Before I wanted to cook something.'

'What was it you wanted to cook.'

'Pigeon. There's a frozen one.'

'You must've been in good spirits.'

Then he falls asleep.

I lay out the shards on the study table. Superglue works only on the larger pieces. When I'm finished, the Japanese fisherman is missing his arms and a piece of his cloak.

To know he'll die and have relief from this.

'Sandro, you used to beat your grandpa at cards because you've got the gift.'

'What gift is that, Bruni.'

'I told you: cards. They're better than horses. With horses, they're in charge, with cards you are.'

'But I don't know how.'

'Sure you do.'

'I don't.'

'It's not like you have to be an expert. Your gift, Sandro. Listen to me. Play one and see how it turns out.'

'One?'

'One.'

'When?'

'I'll find out and give you the good word.'

In the morning I no longer feel any uneasiness about him: I don't wonder if it will happen today, tomorrow, weeks from now. For the past few days I've been waking up and turning my eyes to the window: blackbirds whistle along with the beacon light that calls from the Adriatic.

I get dressed and try to get him to eat. One biscuit, three sips of tea. He makes it to the bathroom on his own, goes back to bed.

I tell him I'd like to go out for an hour before the nurse arrives. 'The sea's covered in mist.'

That pleases him. 'Tell it I said hello.'

When I get back the nurse isn't there yet. I took a round-about way to stay out as long as I could: stopped by a newsstand and then Bar Zeta, where I got a tuna and egg sandwich on a brioche bun and ate it there, paging through the *Gazzetta dello Sport*.

I bring him the Bologna paper and give him my report: the gloomy riptide and the mist and Gattei who's got enormous.

'You saw Gattei Filippo?'

'No, the architect.'

He cocks his head sceptically. He asks if I saw anyone collecting Venus clams. I lie and say lots of people were, and he closes his eyes and I can tell he's imagining the sea slime: that's what he calls the salt film on the shore in the early morning. A stickiness, before the feet sink in, with the soot of dawn on the water's skin and the seagulls soaring mutely overhead. Who knows why the seagulls in Rimini never scream.

And you can tell he's wishing he could go down to the marina, take off his shirt and drape it over one shoulder, tuck his slides into the waistband of his trousers and walk along the water's edge.

'You at the beach, Nando?'

He nods, eyes still closed, and I brush the bottom of his foot with my palm: sea slime, I say.

His blows, when he hit me on the night of the broken Japanese fisherman: weak, precise, mean. I touch my shoulder, there where he punched me as I tried to carry him to bed. Raging against his death sentence.

That afternoon I'm asked about a consulting gig for a men's hair-loss shampoo. They're rebranding and planning a radio and television campaign. They've developed a hair-thickening protein structure, have eliminated parabens, will change their packaging from red to white. They ask me to be onsite in Milan, but I make it clear that I'm out of town and can only videoconference.

We settle on a day and time. It's one of my specialities: the male. I work well on men because I work well on loss. The mane-less lion, the will to control, the urge to flee decline: in advertising, the male is what's called an 'excitable target'.

The nurse's name is Amedeo and at thirty he's already the father of two. He tells us this as if it were a character reference. He prepares to hook up the IV.

Nando studies him. 'Why'd you have two?'

'What do you care,' I interject.

'I wanted a boy and a girl.' Amedeo fiddles with the drip tube. He's muscular but slight, and his cheeks have a girlish pallor. He's about to lift Nando up.

Nando holds on to his neck with both hands. 'Did you get a boy and a girl?'

He says no, mid-lift, with the embarrassment of one who has confessed a weakness. He eases him back on to the bed, the way one lays a newborn in the cradle.

'What did it feel like when the cards were being dealt.'

'In what sense.'

'How did you feel, in that moment.'

'Calm.'

'Calm?'

'Calm. Eager.'

'Curious.'

'Eager.'

'Explain.'

'Like when someone hands you a wrapped gift.'

'Aflutter.'

'Like if someone tells you there's a beautiful ruin you can buy for a song and renovate. But then you have to get in there and renovate it.'

'But that'd be hard work.'

'So is playing cards.'

'Playing cards is hard work?'

'Yeah.'

'And once you pick up the cards?'

'Then I know what to do.'

'And you knew right away if it was a lost cause?'

'You just can't let anyone else see.'

'That's the beginnings of a bluff.'

'Exactly.'

'And what kind of hand would you have when you'd try a lost-cause bluff?'

'No kind of hand.'

'Nothing at all?'

'Nothing at all.'

He shuts up. 'So why would you try it?'

'It's something you try, a bluff – that's it.'

'Because you're trying in general.'
'And you, why'd you fall in love with Mum?'
'Dunno. Because it was her.'
'Exactly.'

After Amedeo leaves he can't sleep. He wants me to get his LPs from the living room. He has about forty: I hold them up one by one and he gives them a yes – that is, worth keeping for later reassessment – or a no, in which case I can do whatever with them. We quibble about Zucchero and Matia Bazar – he's lukewarm on both. Patty Pravo and Venditti are pretty secure. The only ones with no debate are Lucio Dalla and Tina Turner: keep them all, keep them forever.
'What about Guccini?'
'Give those to Don Paolo.'

She was the one who pushed for Guccini. And for their Saturday nights out, at first. And for their dancing sprees. He struggled to separate himself from Caterina's world and find his own way. I came up with a secret nickname for him, my first year in Milan, while I was working on an ad for Barnum & Bailey: the Tamed Man.
His was a docile destiny. One that left the centre stage to others, the shiny shoes, the crazy pursuits. Especially after his heart attack. Their mutual friends, at dinner, would turn first to her, would argue only with her.
I'm nine when I hear her yell: so save it then, this Bar America, little Nando from Ravenna.
Little Nando from Ravenna.
But then came the dancing.

At dawn he's not in his room. He's not in the kitchen, he's not in the bathroom. He's not in the living room. He's in the garden. He has dragged the navy and white chair over and is sitting in it. He has his trowel and is scratching a little canal towards the olive tree.

'You're cold.'

'The squash, remember, in pairs. One on one side and one on the other.'

'Give me that, you're cold.'

'And the vines should be pruned in January. And sink the spade in nice and deep.'

'C'mon, let's go.'

He says no and when he looks up at me his face is the same as always. I leave him be, go back and get a tartan blanket from the garage and lay it on the arm of his chair. I stop at the corner of the wall: he's so thin that even from the back he looks like he's in profile.

The gig for the hair-loss shampoo doesn't come through. They wanted a regular presence in Milan for brainstorming sessions.

I'm also worried about the university job: I may lose the term because I can't guarantee I'll be in residence. I call and they reassure me that I can postpone the start of my course by a month. Instead of two days a week spread over the entire term, I can offer a five-day-a-week intensive.

I end the call and turn my phone over in my hands, rereading Bibi's text: *I'll take you out for dinner at Walter's, how about it? An evening in French blue.*

93

Bibi's French blue. She's convinced I managed to seduce her because I wore a blazer of that colour on our second date. A French-blue blazer is all it takes? A French-blue blazer, and big hands.

I put it on but one of the sleeves is dirty, so I think of the teal boiled-wool overcoat I wore in college, which still fits. I take it out of the wardrobe and put it on and go to his room to say bye. He studies me. He grips his backrest to pull himself up, shoves Amedeo away when he swoops in to help, and falls on to his side. From there he keeps staring at me, and I realise my left pocket flap is badly tucked. I'm about to fix it, but instead I move closer so he can do it with two fingers.

I'm seven and we're in the hardware store by Ponte di Tiberio. He's getting helped by a guy at the end of the paint aisle. There's this display stand by the till with a dozen key rings, each bearing the emblem of a car company: Ferrari, Lamborghini, Porsche, Fiat, Alfa Romeo. I reach out and take the Alfa – it has a satin finish with red inlays. I hold it in my hand, tuck it into my jeans. He returns with the guy, gets the brushes and roller bagged up, pays, and we leave.

For the whole ride home my pocket feels heavy and precious, and as soon as we're back I go into my room, close the door and take out the key ring. To get away with it my first time... If I'd been caught, would the rest still have begun?

Her court: a flood of judgements. Speaking of some guy: bah. Speaking of some woman: bah. Don't be like what's-her-name. Don't be like what's-his-name. You're better than what's-his-name. Worse than what's-her-name. She would swell with self-righteousness.

And he: face twisted, lips tight, as she carried on. Only in the latter days would he blurt: 'God and Mary, Caterina.'

'What do they have to do with anything?'

'They gave you that mouth to talk.'

I go out to meet up with Bibi. I don't think about him during brief outings: supermarket, pharmacy, newsstand. When I stay out longer I'm visited by images of his dimly lit room, his heel tapping the base of the bed, his bony profile. This time I think of his forelock: it splits his forehead down the middle.

I get to Walter's early. Summer's forgotten but he's holding out, doing what he can with mushroom heaters on the veranda. Bibi emerges from the dusk, scarf up to her eyes, which fix on my coat. She's looking for me but I duck my head and then she unwraps her scarf and turns towards the canal with its little tarp-covered boats. Then she comes over, wedges her face under my chin and we stand like that for a while.

After dinner we go to her house and fuck and she can tell I'm in a bad way and lets me go ahead. Afterwards she takes my temples between her palms and holds them until the tears stop.

With Bibi, too, I play the game of being younger and a million euros richer. She wants to know what answers he gave: with his father in the field in Ravenna, the real Tina Turner singing in his living room.

'Me in Bormio, camping with my grandmother, when I was fourteen.'

'Your grandmother took you camping?'

'In a cabin.'

'What about the money?'

'A million now or two billion then?'

'Don't you start too.'

'Be clear.'

'A million now.'

'In that case: I'll buy a house in Canada. A marble bath and a forest view.'

'And quit your job?'

'Not at all. They've got a hundred and fifty-eight species of braconids for me to put under the microscope.'

She gets dressed again. She doesn't ask but it's clear she wants me to leave. She tosses me my T-shirt and stays at the back of the bedroom.

'Take him to Ravenna,' she says quietly. 'To the field where he was with his father.'

When I get home he's awake. Amedeo is in the kitchen making notes in his log: nothing unusual. He tried to convince Nando to reattach the morphine pump, but he wouldn't hear of it. Instead, he asked for a nappy of his own accord and emptied himself with laxatives. They watched *Match Point* and neither fell asleep.

'We weren't convinced by the ending.'

'No ending ever convinces him.'

'You ever see *Match Point*?'

I nod.

'I mean, come on, the investigators know she was pregnant when she was killed. That's motive to arrest the lover for murder, right?'

He heads towards the door, then comes back into the kitchen and opens the cabinet where we keep the medicine. There are two new vials.

'This one's for severe pain – thirty drops on top of the fentanyl. Today I gave him about fifteen. This other one is to help him sleep, forty drops.'

After he's gone, Nando calls me. He overheard our conversation.

'It's obvious even to the police that the lover's guilty.' His voice is croaky and he reaches for his glass of water. 'How can you not arrest him?'

I lie down next to him. 'You know, Nando, I like this Bibi.'

The good word from Bruni came one Wednesday: he had a table for me.

'A table?'

'Cards, Sandro.'

The appointment was for Saturday, in a condo with a big oleander in front, in Rimini's Padulli neighbourhood, west of Ina Casa. A hundred euros, with chips, cool people. He would be there too.

'You're really going too?'

'I have to.'

'You're playing?'

'The masters of ceremony don't play.'

'A hundred euros is the most I can lose?'

Then Bruni said to me: You'll do well, you'll see.

He stands on his own in the morning. He asks for his after-shave sweater and wants to put it on by himself. For the sweatpants he accepts a little help around the ankles. He also wants shoes; I tie them for him.

'How're you feeling today?'

'Yes, today yes.'

At breakfast, his back is stiff, his face ashen. He eats a shortbread biscuit and drinks tea on his feet, leaning against the counter. He studies the dishes heaped by the sink. 'It's all a-jumble.' He takes in the glasses, the spice jars, the stove. 'Lemme see,' he says, pointing at the box of matches.

'What.'

'If you're any good at it.'

I put away the shortbread and the teapot, wash my cup and dry it. I reach for the box of matches, extract one and swipe it, and the head ignites.

'You're good.'

The flame dies halfway down the stick but he keeps staring as if it were still lit. Then he comes over and takes out a new match. He lifts it to his face, eyeing the stick, the head, as if looking for imperfections, then leaves the kitchen with it. He goes into the hall, towards the stairs. He goes down the first step and I offer him my arm until we reach the front door. I go off and when I return with jackets, he's outside in his tracksuit. I cover him and we cross the open space in front of the garage, turn the corner, and come to the vegetable garden. He stops in front of the cabbage. He drops into the chair, his hair a scrawl atop his head.

He's still holding the match between his thumb and finger. He tries to light it against the arm of the chair, drops it, bends down to retrieve it. I bend down too and hand it to him and when he takes it he's crying. His eye sockets are purple and the autumn smells of wood, as it did when I was a boy and the men would stack firewood before the first frost. I dab at one cheek, feel the heat of his breath. 'Let's go to Ravenna, Nando. I'll take you to San Zaccaria.'

'The garden, Sandrin,' he sniffs. 'Burn the garden.'

I preferred chips and avoided cash games: the naked brutality of the stakes. I avoided venues where multiple games were played at once. I avoided the Texas variant: its players were children of the internet, often indifferent to the appeal of a tight circle. I kept track of the schedule for this dizzying Milan: all those people, their inertia helping to hide their wait for a date at the table.

When I could, I'd ask if they would have the green felt: the feel of it on the sides of my hands, the friction on my wrists when I check my cards.

He doesn't take his eyes off the part of the garden next to the grapevine.

'Let's go to San Zaccaria, Nando.'

He looks at me bewildered. 'To San Zaccaria.'

'Yeah.'

'They redid the road.'

I wipe his other cheek too. It's cold. I lay my palm against it and hold it there. I help him up and walk him to the front of the house.

'Best not to go to San Zaccaria, Sandro.'

'Whatever you want.'

He looks towards the garage. 'Okay, let's go.'

'Nòna Biènca.'

Nòna Biènca was an old lady everyone in Rimini used to know. To every question she'd answer no, which then became yes. You want some watermelon? No. Okay fine, a small slice. Coming to the beach? No. Maybe just a little while. Shall we have dinner with the uncles? No. What time should I come? And so on. She had white hair and I don't know how many grandchildren.

'Eight grandchildren,' he says as soon as we merge on to the Adriatica towards Ravenna. He sprawls among pillows and with two fingers rubs the ashtray and glove compartment. They're polished to a shine, like the gear knob, like the instrument panel and the floor mats: we had the Renault 5 washed at the Q8 gas station on Via Marecchiese, bought a check blanket and fixed the red knob on the radio.

'But the real Nòna Biènca was your mum,' he says.

'Saturdays?'

'Always. But not only Saturdays.'

'I remember the Saturdays. Are you going dancing, Mum? No, I'm not.'

'And she always ended up on the dance floor.'

He falls quiet and so do I, and we approach Cervia in a well-oiled silence we both enjoy.

Then he tells me that one afternoon being Nòna Biènca saved him.

'How so?'

'With a woman.'

'How so?'

'I was about to be a yes and then I was a no.'

We're skirting Cervia.

'Was Mum already in the picture?'

He pulls himself up and brings his face to the window to see the salt pans. The road is a tongue and it cuts across the lagoons as we head inland. He's dozing off. His legs sway on the curves – all that tap and waltz and gunslinger music.

He pulls himself up again two hundred metres from the sign that says 'S. ZACCARIA (District of Ravenna)'. He peers down the road that forks off into the village – nine hundred souls and now his. He's alert, a mongoose on the prowl, holding the grab handle above the door and craning his neck to get glimpses of the farmyards, the bar with old men behind the window, the war memorial, the CRAI supermarket that when he was a kid was a dairy that had sugar wafers.

He asks to slow down in front of the Circolo dei Repubblicani. It looks the same as always only more washed out, the windows and front door peeling but intact, the party's ivy-leaf symbol on the façade above.

'Aurelio Pagliarani': he utters his father's first and last names and smiles. There's nothing bitter about it, it's just a memory, and his eyes remain fixed on the ivy-leaf and on his thoughts: his father, two weeks after taking office as the newly elected chairman of the party's local chapter, discovers that some dues have gone missing. Aurelio Pagliarani reports their absence. It's not a lot of money, no one is accused of anything – a small oversight, an error in the inherited accounts.

'He couldn't rest. He went over those records morning and night, or took to the fields to take his frustrations out on the spade.' He smacks his saliva. 'Six months later he was in his coffin.'

We reach Via del Sale. They lived halfway down, in the big house with the green shutters. I pull up to the iron gate: it's been empty since they sold it to a neighbour. The grass is tall and two combines and a tractor sit in the yard. The well is overgrown with vines; beyond it the field begins.

'That's where I was with my dad.' He points. It's ploughed and dry. 'That's where we'd hitch the buggy to that white filly with Mamma on Sundays.'

'What about the orchard?'

He shifts his finger to the east, beyond the shed where they kept the farm machinery and the livestock scales. Instead of peach trees they've planted apples, which are head high and stretch to the drainage ditch. He pinches the air between his fingers: a Romagnolo tailor mending a memory.

Bruni was waiting for me outside the building with the big oleander in front. We went up to the door and I pulled out my hundred euros. Relax, Sandro. He introduced me to the others.

'Gentlemen, the man with the gift.'

But I didn't win. I mostly defended my hundred, losing only seven euros. Then I stayed and watched the others play and drank a couple of amaros. Late in the day I said goodbye and left the oleander house.

And on the street I said it to myself: I'm doing well.

He doesn't want to stop at the San Zaccaria cemetery. We cruise past, and as we leave the village behind he falls asleep. He sleeps, he wakes, sleeps and wakes, Milano Marittima, Cervia, Cesenatico: he names them each time he opens his eyes and recognises where we are. Before gliding down the sloping road towards Rimini he says he'd like to see the beach.

'Wouldn't tomorrow be better?'

'Tell me about this Bibi.'

We're quiet then, the Renault 5 hissing loudly as we enter the town, and he hunkers against his door until we reach the port.

He pulls himself up, looks at me. 'Does she laugh?'

'What?'

'Bibi.'

'She laughs and laughs.'

'What's her laugh like?'

'She has a dimple here,' I say, touching his left cheek as I park near the Palata. They've taken down the Ferris wheel, and the fishing boats are docked even though it's afternoon.

'How is that possible?'

He slumps back against the headrest.

'Must've had a good catch.'

'How's it possible, your mum and me, that month we'd spend, off season, dancing every night. Our scaramàz.'

'Arnica cream for your sore legs.'

He stretches his neck back and then forward again. 'We had dance, Sandrin. You had cards.'

'What I had was something else.'

He scratches his chin. 'We'll all be free in the end, right?'

A fishing boat foams at the stern as men untie it from the bollard and I roll down the window and sing *Aria di mar arriva a me e non te ne andar.* He looks over at me, a blazon of light stamped on his forehead.

Aren't I better – aren't we better? Isn't my pussy better? And the time we were going to spend in Lisbon, wasn't that going to be better? *Better* was the last word between us.

When Giulia discovered the deficit in our joint account, I didn't make her any promises – she no longer wanted any promises from me. She came to get her things while I was at work.

Did she really wear her hair in a bob? When we first met, her hair was shoulder length. Or maybe neither is true. Her hair was brown, it was jet black. The sleek hands of a pianist: she had played because her mother wanted her to. She came up to my chest, or my throat. And her nose, her mouth – what were they like? She had a mole on one cheekbone. Giulia, the ghost.

Ghosts. Her, the ones before her, and my friends, my colleagues, strangers on the street, acquaintances – even the guys in Rimini. They melt into air. But off to one side, crystal clear, the table and those of us around it. The players.

We sit in the car facing the Palata. The fishing boats are gone now and no one's around but a little ice-cream truck and the seagulls on the anchor memorial.

Turns out he'd rather be on holiday. And where would you like to be on holiday? He's not sure, so I tell him we're in Sardinia. We've already been to Sardinia. How about Salento? Yes, Salento, yes – and how old are we? Twenty-one, Nando. Why twenty-one precisely? Twenty-one. I touch his head as I tell him we're wearing Panama hats and I touch his shoulders as I tell him we're wearing short-sleeved shirts. Cigarettes in our shirt pockets? Yes, cigarettes in our shirt pockets, because we're the vitelloni of Salento. He leans towards the fogged-up window, swipes a hand to clear it, and turns to me: And who's better with the girls, Sandrin? You are for now, but I'm hard on your heels and I'll catch you eventually.

He laughs, then coughs.

Then I say, 'We're in Rimini, Nando: we're on holiday in Rimini. With all those German girls and dance halls.'

'All those dance halls.'

They discovered the first shortfall in 2007: two hundred euros missing from their safe. They talked about it at dinner in my presence. We must've counted wrong, Caterina. Yeah, we must've counted wrong, Nando, what a couple of dummies. So I decided not to give it back.

Two weeks later I borrowed three hundred, returning it the morning after the game. Two months later, eight hundred more, returned the morning after. A week later, another three hundred, returned the next morning. Then two hundred more, and one hundred, and six hundred. All returned the next morning, or within six days at most. Then I lost four thousand at a game in Pesaro, nine hundred of which was theirs. I wasn't able to return it.

I waited; they never said a word. I was making fourteen hundred euros a month at the time, and I tightened my belt for two months, saved a thousand. I took that to a medium-stakes table and left with fifty-two hundred. It was too late to return the nine hundred from Pesaro. But I did.

That evening they came to my room: 'Sandro.'

Later a trimaran returns to the harbour and he rolls his window down and sticks a hand out as if to wave. He opens and closes his fingers to catch the breeze.

'You'll get cold.'

'Say hello to Montescudo for me.'

But I'm not sure I heard right, and when I don't reply he turns to me: 'Say hello for me.'

'We'll go back.'

'That stone we picked up at the church. It's by the tool shed, under the wheelbarrow and the ivy – don't forget. It's a turtle.'

'It's too long to make a turtle.'

He mumbles something I can't make out. He waits for me to lean in and repeats it: 'It's by the tool shed, okay?'

I nod.

'I got it for you.'

He leans back in the seat, signals that he wants to go home. We get there quickly and I have a feeling it will be his last night.

I take him to bed and change him, button his pyjamas. I bring the blanket up to his stomach, take his foot and pull it slowly towards the edge. I let it hang over the side. I stay there on my knees.

I bluffed hard only once: on Via Maroncelli, on the third floor of the building with putti on the gate. Milan in January: crumpled like wrapping paper and hidden by thick banks of fog.

There are five of us at the table: cash in hand or guaranteed within two days, four thousand to sit. Joining me: another direct referral, an occasional player vouched for by reliable sources, a fish, and a chameleon playing for the first time in Milan.

The fish is an accountant who, after becoming an accountant, inherited a small pharmaceutical company near Piacenza: never complains, always pays, always loses, always receives the red-carpet treatment. The chameleon is a classic Milanese blowhard in his mid-forties, son of a lawyer who passed the vice down to him: his father vouches for him, if indirectly, which is enough because he's still in the organisation. Without the blood guarantee someone in the organisation would have had to present him, as happened with me: my CEO, a financial advisor who founded the ad agency where I work, took a liking to me because I won him an advertising competition for herbicides in my first year on the job. Esteem, trust, dinners in Milan, dinner at his home in Monza with his wife and Giulia, and so on.

The other referral is a former football coach. The occasional player is a guy who moved to London and made a fortune with an investment fund: he's friendly, always on the verge of a smile, his shirt a size too big, his hair in a crew cut.

They deal the cards and I have nothing in my hand. After the draw, still nothing. It's obvious that the fish has something in the works because he raises eagerly, and strangely the Londoner and the chameleon both fold in quick succession. I suspect the three of arranging to let the accountant win in exchange for a cut. The former coach has figured it out and he too folds quickly.

I'm at a crossroads: fold or go for the rabbit punch, the big bluff. The rabbit punch can work if it develops naturally. The only way to do it is by not thinking too much about doing it: raise with minimal pauses, no rushing and no dawdling. Look strong, control your cards, set them down and keep them there, manage your chips, which means pushing them into the pot without theatrics.

The pot rises to ten thousand three hundred: the fish and I raise and reraise. I imagine we're building an Inca temple and each raise is another brick. It's an image that estranges and displaces me from my context: I look calm, my expression doesn't change, my cheeks don't flush.

I keep going until the Inca temple I'm visualising is three-quarters done: I take advantage of the desire to see it fully completed by calling as soon as the fish raises. I don't hesitate because I want the temple to be finished. The pot is now over eighteen thousand.

I'm in, the fish is in, the Inca temple is complete, and it's time to show our cards. Before I do, I wonder how I'll fill the hole I've dug for myself: they'll ask my CEO for the shortfall and he'll take it out of my salary and I'll have to go to Rimini for more.

We turn the cards over: he has nothing either. But my ace-queen beats his ace-jack. I take home almost nineteen thousand euros.

The next day Giulia says: You're gambling.

Leg hanging off the bed, ankle bone stamped with blue veins. I'm the one keeping him here – empty, rasping. Mourning the fact that I can't mourn him yet.

We had never got around to removing his name from my current account. After the money went missing from the safe he went to the bank and had them print a list of my transactions. An average of twenty-six withdrawals a month for the previous seventeen months, substantial cash deposits every forty days. As the branch manager said: a cash flow worthy of a small business.

He doesn't breathe well in the night: extended apneas, air whistling from his lips, gurgling.

He starts to moan: a whine that snakes out of his mouth and back in, an animal song in the forest.

He shifts in his bed, raising his shoulders, lowering them, raising them. I call his name, the moaning starts again, I call his name.

Before dawn he whips the nightstand with his arm. The bedside lamp falls to the carpet and his arm dangles down. His eyelids are closed and his breath is a hiss. On his wrist a dark blot: blood.

I tend to it, he doesn't move, mutters something. Saliva trickles towards his neck, I dry it and adjust his pillow, shifting his position so that his arms are down by his sides. He moves one away.

'Nando, you're good now.'

He moves the other one too.

His eyes open mid-morning and scan the room until they find me. He looks at the plaster on his wrist, turns towards the nightstand. Looks at the plaster again, calming as I pull up his sheet.

'What is it I'm doing here.'

'It's okay.'

'And how could your mum have done that.'

'Done what.'

'Gone before me.'

I change his plaster because the blood has soaked through. 'She told us she would, in Montescudo, the night of the fireflies – remember?'

He nods that he does.

I nudge his forelock off his forehead. 'She learned it from those cards of hers. You remember that evening.'

'Caterina… I remember it was getting dark and there were fireflies.'

She made a beeline for the basement and found me. I was no longer a child, but it was before Giulia, and they had discovered I had raided their safe.

'Muccio, you there?' She clicked open the folding door and heard me in the corner behind the coat rack. Without turning the light on she groped her way forward, sat on the low shoe bench. We stayed like that, our breaths shallow, the silence deeper than silence – at one point she even stopped breathing. Then I barked at her that she had to leave, and when I was alone I clung to the jackets hanging on the coat rack, and I needed to tell them: Mamma.

His side is bothering him and he tries to sit up but can't. He lies back down and turns his head the other way. He starts to retch. I put the bucket under him – nothing comes out. He rolls back on to the pillow. I wipe his moustache.

I phone Amedeo: he says I should call the hospice people right away. He'll come by in the morning, but I am to let him know if muscle contractions start.

'What kind of contractions.'

'Spasms, jerks. Sometimes the muscles move without him meaning to. I'll be there at eight in the morning.' His voice is a whistle.

'Come now.' Mine's a whistle too.

'What?'

'Now.'

'I can't now.'

I press the phone into my ear. 'I can't do this, Amedeo.'

'I'm at the hospital.'

'I can't do this.'

The softest whistle: 'Tonight around nine. I'll come for a couple of hours.'

'I cannot do this.'

At the table: to seem to be one thing and be another. Is that the gift?

I notify the hospice service. They arrive in a pair again. The man examines him as I stay on the end of the bed. The woman informs me that they're adding morphine on top of the fentanyl. After they administer it his face slackens, but before sleep comes he manages to say: Don Paolo.

The hospice people are still there when Don Paolo arrives. He stands in the doorway, sees that he's sleeping and waits until the pair leave.

He enters quietly, approaches haltingly, sits beside him and touches his cheek to Nando's. He caresses him without touching him. Then he raises a hand, and he blesses him.

The table in Via Cartoleria in Bologna decided I would keep playing. There were four of us, I sat down with nine hundred euros in cash. One round and I'm done, that was my promise: and I played brashly, as in certain farewells. Instead I won four thousand and eighty.

Amedeo shows up before nine. I hear them murmuring in the bedroom.

When he joins me in the kitchen he puts his backpack on the table, opens it and pulls out the DVD of *Fight Club*. 'Your dad picked the crazy guys.'

'Really?'

'He could've picked *Minority Report* or *The Matrix*.'

'Not what I expected from you.'

'What did you expect?'

'Dunno. *Notting Hill*?'

He stares at me over his glasses. 'Go on, take off.'

The first thrashing was in an apartment in central Milan, overlooking a petrol station. We were all rounded up at the last minute.

I hear a TV in the background. Before we start I go to the window and look out: streetlights around the Agip sign, a white pigeon resting on the petrol station roof. It feels like a good omen.

The pot is four thousand and change. I have a pair of ladies in my hand. I play warily but at one point raise because I feel like it. We get to eleven thousand three hundred. I decide to raise again: I push my stack of chips into the pot with my index finger and thumb; my little finger is slightly extended and twitches, and I bring it in so as not to bump the other chips. Then my hand withdraws, in an overly cautious motion: slow, tentative, aborted, leaving my chips apart from the others. Overly cautious: now they know my cards are weak.

I hold course and wait for the next round of betting, raising quickly to compensate. I have too much in the pot to fold now: they know that too and reraise quickly. And again. The pot is over fifteen thousand. It makes no sense to fold now – but I do. I get up and go back to the window: the pigeon is still there. At the table there are three more raises, then they show their cards: the first lays down a total bluff. The other lays down a pair of sevens. I would have more than sixteen thousand in my pocket.

I wait for Amedeo to start *Fight Club* before going outside and into the garage. We've kept the keys to the Renault 5 in the empty jar of white spirit since 1994. I grab them, start the engine and pull out. He must be pricking up his ears, perhaps pleased for his Milva to get a surprise outing. Milva: the name he gave her at some point because she matches the singer's famous red hair.

I drive towards the old ramparts and the bypass, past the hospital – Rimini in the plain glow of its off-season lights. I arrive at Bibi's apartment building and ring her bell.

She's worried because she wasn't expecting me, and she keeps worrying even after we sit on the sofa and I reassure her.

We drink a beer and watch a bit of *The Crown*. The wall behind the TV is covered with comic strips and photos: her among iguanas in the Galápagos, her upside down during an acrobat class, the border collie she had as a girl, India ink lithographs of exotic insects.

I fuck her hard, squeezing her neck.

'Hey,' she says when we're done.

'I have to go home.'

But I don't go home. I take the waterfront road down through Marina Centro to Miramare and back up, betting that the Renault won't shriek at the Grand Hotel roundabout. I keep it above seventy, the wheels squealing and the steering wheel light, and I don't cut a single corner.

I reach Piazza Tripoli and slow down in front of the sweetshop, whose blinds are still up: packets of licorice hang from the ceiling, along with marshmallows and clusters of strawberry jelly sweets. A Pakistani man is mopping the floor and glancing at a wall-mounted television. Once upon a time the people of Rimini had their children to run these seaside shops, during the summer and even after summer was over – perhaps in the evening when the parents were tired and needed help finishing the day and rolling down the blinds. Then the parents retired and the kids moved out of town for work, leaving the beachfront to outsiders and to premature hibernation.

I loop around Piazza Tripoli, park in front of the church, and switch off the engine and radio. The shops here are all closed, and at the beginning of October the dance hall turned back into a cinema. The sign is now lit: Atlantide.

I lean my head back against the seat. Cowboys, I say. And my voice in the cockpit is metal: cowboys.

I started playing for high stakes two years after my baptism at the oleander condo. It's 2005, I'm at a table in Cesena: you need at least two grand to sit. It's Christmastime. A call from Bruni in mid-afternoon, a few hours to think about it: I say yes. I win fifty-two hundred with three of a kind and do something I'll never do again: I show my joy, raising a clenched fist.

Winning when you play at the big table for the first time draws a line: thirty-seven per cent of these happy debutants will become hooked on the game. Most are hyperfrontal, so called after the area of the brain activated by adrenal stimuli. Symptoms of this activation appear within half a minute of the stimulus: sternal pressure, tremors in the inside of the elbow, dry mouth, palpitations, increased skin conductance. It's just like falling in love.

I leave Piazza Tripoli again and go back to the Pakistani guy's sweetshop. I buy some gummy crocodiles and chocolate lentils, eat them like peanuts. They're gone before I'm back in the driver's seat.

I gun the Renault 5 all the way home. When I get there, the engine hasn't shrieked once and the kitchen light is on. I go up and find Amedeo writing in his log at the table. He informs me that breath during sleep is erratic, a normal occurrence that can be frightening at times. '*Fight Club* put him to sleep. *Notting Hill* might've been better.' He gets up from his chair, tears off a paper towel and wipes sugar off my mouth. 'Thrilling night for you too, I see.'

'Did he ask for me?'

He shakes his head as he puts his ammo belt of blister packs and vials in order. He's so precise that he orients each label so it can be read at a glance.

'Amedeo.'

'Yeah.'

'Thank you.'

He puts his jacket on. 'At night he closes his eyes and dances. That's what he told me this evening.'

He says goodbye and leaves the house and gets into his car: his tenderness with the accelerator of his Toyota Yaris, for fear of waking him.

That erratic breath during sleep. It gets stranded in his diaphragm, dissolving every other time his chest expands.

'I'm here,' I whisper. 'It's me.'

He doesn't move.

'I'm here.' I squeeze his arm and he falls back to sleep. I sit in the rattan chair, doze, wake. Around midnight his breath evens again and his body relaxes.

I move to my room, undress, put on my sweatshirt: I listen to him from my bed. He snores and every three or four breaths he goes into apnea, then breathes in again. I'm about to fall asleep when a breath makes him cough and I get up.

I go back to his room and approach him. His chest is rising and falling, his profile is catching the light from the hall. His right foot, still outside the blanket, is catching the cool air.

I lie down beside him, he disappears under the covers. We sleep.

I wake near dawn: he's in the same position and I think of my mother and I clutch the headboard behind me – maybe she used to clutch it too, how many times has it been clutched.

I'm eleven and it's summer. He and I are at the beach, around eight in the evening. She's at her painting class. He liked to get pizza from the kiosk on the promenade and take it back to our umbrella to eat. We're walking along, cutting across the empty beach, when we notice some T-shirts on a lounge chair, and on the T-shirts a pair of regular glasses and a pair of sunglasses. After we pass, he stops and turns back towards the shirts and glasses. The sunglasses are Persols, he says, the folding kind. He looks around: there's no one but the lifeguards, who are starting to close up, working in from the water. He walks to the lounge chair and takes the sunglasses. Signals for me to get moving. I walk with my head down, my feet too long and his veiny, struggling to keep up, the pocket of his shorts bulging.

We arrive at the kiosk, order, get our pizzas boxed, and return along the promenade. We take the boardwalk back to Bagno 41 and our beach umbrella. Before we sit he pulls the Persols out of his pocket and balls them up in a towel, which he hides in the beach bag. Then we start eating, and I look for the lounge chair with the T-shirts: it's twenty metres away at an angle. I eat and occasionally glance over, until a woman and a girl come up from the water and walk to it. They pick up towels and the girl kneels down and picks up her glasses, puts them on. The woman dries her hair, bends down and lifts up the T-shirts, bends further down, looking under and around the shirts. The girl starts looking too.

'Eat your pizza, Sandro.'

I eat my pizza and watch as the woman and girl go over to the lifeguard. They talk, towels and T-shirts draped on their forearms. Then they turn towards us.

'They're coming,' I say in a mutilated voice.

'Eat your pizza.'

I take a sip of my Coke, he drinks from his beer and says he's still thinking about Schillaci's goal last night against Uruguay, a beautiful goal, and meanwhile the woman is approaching, trailing the girl behind her.

She nods at us: 'Good evening.'

'Good evening.'

'Did you happen to see anyone around that umbrella?' She's pointing.

I shake my head.

He mumbles, 'We just got back from the pizza place, I'm sorry.'

'I had some sunglasses and now they're gone.'

'I'm sorry.' His slice is drooping from his hand.

'Thanks anyway.' She waves, and so do we, and the girl, who's been standing motionless, finally follows.

We don't talk, we take bites, he sets his piece down on its box and washes his bite down with a sip of beer.

'That Schillaci goal, eh?' he says.

I want to go home but we hold off for five minutes so as not to arouse suspicion. Then we get up, toss the boxes and cans in the bin and head to the car. He drives slowly back towards Ina Casa, parks in our courtyard and turns off the engine. He drums his fingers on the steering wheel.

'Hey, Sandrin, weren't we lucky to have found these folding Persols in the sand?'

And now he pulls them out and tries them on.

He gasps at dawn. Then stops breathing. I shake him, he gasps again, I lift him into a sitting position. 'Oh,' I shout and lay him back down, about to call the ambulance. He's staring at me but doesn't see me.

'Nando' – I have an arm around his neck – 'Nando.' I push his forelock off his forehead. Breath wisps from his mouth.

He used to get a rash on his shoulders when she danced with other men.

'Sounds like a joke,' I said when she confided it to me. She laughed and made me promise never to bring it up around him. I promised, but on Sunday mornings I would look for red patches around his neck.

'You should only dance with him,' I told her.

'He doesn't go for the Caribbean dances.'

Breath is still wisping up from his lungs. It's me, it's Sandro. His eyelids move. It's me, and outside I think that's a blackcap chirping.

One of his hands is holding one of mine and the other is clawing the sheet. His breath is gravelly. I take his other hand, it's warm, and he digs his ring finger into one of my knuckles. He squeezes the sleeve of my sweatshirt, lifts his head.

'Sandro.'

'Dad.'

Stolen from God: his phrase against the doggedness of fate. We heard it through his teeth as we were coming back from his mother's funeral.

'What did you steal from God?' Don Paolo was in the passenger seat.

'He wants to keep you here to suffer, and we end it sooner than planned.'

'Then you're stealing from yourself.'

'Explain.'

'If God has chosen that you should suffer a little, there must be a reason.'

'What a load.'

'The passion of Christ then?'

'Passion my arse. Mamma suffered. And Dad before her. And Christ suffered.'

'And what was it you wanted to do for your mamma? Let's hear it.'

'What do you know about it.'

'Let's hear it. What was it you wanted to do?'

'If I was a doctor or a nurse.' We were driving between the salt pans, his head pushed back on his headrest and his arms straight on the steering wheel.

'What was it you wanted to do, eh, smart guy?' Don Paolo insisted.

He took the road towards Cervia.

Then dawn is over and we're lying down. I have one hand around his wrist. He's scratching me with his little finger, pausing, starting up again. He's looking at the ceiling, the plaster she wanted, a floral motif with cornucopias at the corners.

I hadn't been playing long. One evening Caterina followed me to the oleander condo, in the Padulli neighbourhood, where Bruni and the others were waiting for me to start a game.

I got out of my car and she got out of hers and came to me and begged me not to go in. I went in, and when I came out at the end of the night she was still there. Did you lose? I won. How much did you win? Six hundred. Tomorrow how much will you lose? Maybe I'll win. You won't, everyone knows people don't win.

On the way home I was the one who followed her, but she kept going, into the city centre. She parked under the old walls. We got out of our cars and walked together along the avenue, in silence. At one point she said I know a specialist who can help you. I broke away and ducked into Bar Giandone, she followed, and we ate ham and mayo sandwiches, shared a Coke. Then she brought up the story of the phone call on the night of Ferragosto. I pretended not to remember.

'That phone call, Sandro. That man with the kind voice who threatened to kill us all over your gambling debts. Your dad crying.'

'You made that up.' I stared at her.

And her, with her mother's grimace.

His rib cage rises and stays up. Should I call Amedeo, hospice care, the doctor? I take out my phone, put it away again. I go to the kitchen for fentanyl and look in the medication box. I take the sleeping drops, a spoon.

I win because I dominate the breaking point. When most would fold, I stay in.

Fentanyl tablet under the tongue. Then thirty drops from the vial on to the spoon. His lips are white. He moves his head as if to extract his neck from a noose.

Lower stakes, fewer games, until it stops: that's the plan. I promise Giulia. I stick to the plan. Three games a month, then two, then none. Giulia asks nothing more, understands the signs: the nerves, the troubled sex, the appetite. I gain six kilos in two and a half months, and when I return to Rimini they too can tell I've got my act together. She says: It's about time. He says nothing. Later he says: *Amaracmànd* – I beg of you.

He coughs to swallow the thirty drops. Thank you, I think I hear him say.

But I start playing again.
    Stop and start again. Hoping, each time, that it will get less traction. Hoping the deck is tired.

The cut on his wrist from his bedside lamp: a brown line now. I stroke it. With his thumb, he scratches me again, but light as an ant, between two fingers.

The bulge of coat pockets after a good game. Leaving the apartment, or the condo, and spilling back into the street, one hand always over the swollen growth of winnings. Looking at passing faces and thinking: I have it and you don't. You and your submissive pockets.

He sleeps. I wait, an hour passes, two, then his eyes open but don't move. He lets out a whistle, his hands flutter, his back arches, and his head slaps the headboard. He stops moving and his rib cage subsides.

Later, at her burial, I swear to her once and for all: I'm quitting.

The way to stop is cold turkey, overnight. To find some compensations. And finally to go back for one last game – and to feel that the deck is tired, the games are over. The countercheck.

I quit cold turkey. Didn't compensate, didn't countercheck. But after the day of my mother's funeral an image persisted: her in her coffin, her body decomposing, her face being borne away along with my vice. Her features dissolving, her materfamilial sweetness crumbling under earth. Her way of disappearing, and my way of disappearing.

Morning is over. His head is tilted back, Adam's apple protruding sharply. His last breath was twenty minutes ago.

November

It's still dark out. He's been dead for sixty-five hours; the funeral was yesterday.

I turn on the lights and open the four sections of his wardrobe. From each I grab armfuls of jackets and trousers, uprooting them with their hangers, and toss them on to the floor. I pick it all up from there and take it in three trips to my room. I do the same with his sweaters, three drawerfuls per section, tossing them to the floor and carrying them to my room, then I move on to the rods on which he hung his belts and ties: toss to the floor, haul away. I clean out his section of nice clothes and the two windbreakers. He never wore gloves.

I clutch, squeeze, convey down the hall, then come back, kneel in front of the antique dresser – woollen vests, long johns, cotton handkerchiefs, underpants – then stand with my arms full and stare at his bed. The sheet that covered him, rolled up in the exact centre of their double bed, the mattress pad with its verdigris stains a shroud: blurry around the back and pelvis, sharp around the legs.

I separate the jackets from the rest. I check the pockets, inside and outside, and when I find something I put it without looking into a plastic bag. Then I find a ticket with sequins sewn on around the edges: the Tre Stelle competition from 30 April 2009: the Stumble.

The Stumble was his term for it: he's dancing the shag at Tre Stelle before a jury of eleven, with seventy watching from tables. For their finale he has to scoot behind her with an angled slide. The moment comes: he draws back, barely touching her, slides two steps over, and as he's about to rise up from the floor his left foot snags on the linoleum. He stumbles, making her stumble too.

After checking the pockets I go through the plastic bag of their contents: tissues, a receipt, a faded cinema ticket, his 2018 Railway Social membership card, a lighter and a pack of chewing gum, a mothball.

I stow the jackets in a box in the hallway, look through the trousers and find a half-full pack of cigarettes and a toothpick.

The aftershave sweater hangs on a chair, one sleeve touching the ground. I pick it up: collar stretched, wool pilled. I sit, fold it neatly, slowly, set it on my lap.

His things. And hers too, still in the wardrobes and the attic and the basement. Let's take them out, Nando, since they hurt you. They'll hurt you, you who are always slipping away.

By the time I roll up the study blinds, it's getting light out. On the table, the wooden chest with francs and pounds, money that friends brought us from their travels (yen, a five-dollar bill, a ten-peso coin), one-hundred and two-hundred lira coins, her third eye pendant, a photo of Gaetano Scirea from the famous snowstorm match between Brescia and Juventus. On the back he has written the date of his father's death: 6 March 1969.

He moved her file box marked 'Muccio' to his desk. Clippings of my ads. It's next to another box, 'Due dates', which holds folders of required paperwork for each month of the year plus a folder for appliance warranties and manuals.

The safe is on a shelf by the window, behind the last two volumes of the Fabbri encyclopaedia. The key has always been in the mayonnaise jar, top shelf of the fridge. Freezing, to be warmed in the hand as I used to do in secret as a boy.

I turn the key. Inside: the three gold coins, the cheque-book, and one thousand six hundred and fifty euros in fifty-euro notes.

Over the course of four years and five months they topped up my bank account eleven times – forty-one thousand euros in all. *Top up* was the phrase that appeared as the transfer description.

When I received them, the following script would play out: I'd phone Rimini in mock protest, But why, What for, I'm giving it back. Then they would recite their lines: You're all we've got, take it and be done with it. Knowing they were feeding my vice.

My drawing from primary school that she was attached to because of the word 'mamma' on the right: she saved it between the two atlases.

Her and her struggle to accept that I would only call her Caterina. And him, Nando. And his ease with his first name in his son's mouth.

The surprise is in the Adidas windbreaker: a cigar. A Toscanello. He never smoked cigars in front of me. I also find ten laundered euros in the parka.

He used to snoop around investigating me; I've become him.

I gather the scarves and close the boxes. I take half of the boxes to the garage, pile them near the workbench. I move them, put them back, move them again. I sit on them. I'm still. The burning descends from my eyes down to my oesophagus and into my lungs. I pull myself up and when I walk outside it's the third morning without him. A magpie is pecking at the bark of the pine, the navy and white chair is over by the wall, dragged by the winds of November.

The shame of his Stumble at Tre Stelle. But they didn't call it shame. Rather: that cazèda, that bullshit: almost funny, a silly thing, a joke not even worth the telling.

And their bodies, from that day on, gradually stiffening, like drying plaster.

I go back to his room. The sheet and the mattress pad: I sit down, they've already lost their smell. I reach a hand to touch them, grasp them. I lean over, lie down, and sobs rise around me.

At the end of the morning Lele and Walter come and find the boxes in the hallway. There are just as many in the garage.

'Waiting for us, huh?'

'I couldn't sleep.'

'Who do we give them to?'

'Don Paolo's guys are coming.'

'That's fucked up. Give it a few days at least.' They're standing behind me as I get busy again, and Walter digs in and tells me not to completely erase the traces. He calls them *traces*, which brings me up short: as if once the clean-up is finished the father will no longer exist.

Then he slips into the living room. Lele follows and sprawls on the sofa, legs stretching into the middle of the carpet. He starts to take off his coat, pauses with his hands at the buttons. 'This is where he practised dancing, isn't it?'

It was here he practised dancing: one night, weeks after the Stumble, he can't sleep and gets out of bed. He comes to the living room, redoes the step that brought them down. He lifts his left foot, hops sideways and lands on the rug. Lifts his left foot, hops sideways and lands. The carpet rippling as she comes in: Nando.

Everyone laughed – Caterina, everyone.

Lele wants to see his room again. On the threshold he crosses himself and stares at the mattress: the piss stain is an upside-down oak. He leads me away, as if I had been the one lingering there. He herds me to the kitchen, shoulder against my back, almost pushing. He sits close to me, tanned from a trip to Lanzarote.

Walter is fumbling in the cupboard. I ask him if he's closed his place for the season yet.

'Next Thursday.' He takes out the moka pot to make coffee. 'You know Nando used to come in all the time.'

'I knew he went in, yeah.'

'In the first month after we opened he came in every night. Next to last stool overlooking the canal. Campari and tonic.'

'Campari and tonic is odd.' Lele is looking at me.

'And arrosticini.' Walter is also looking at me. Then together they go into the hallway and carefully organise the boxes. They arrange them efficiently, putting them all in one row against the wall, the open ones on top. 'We think you want to keep at least one of Nando's jackets.'

'Maybe.'

'Consider it. And now let's go.'

'Go where?'

They don't answer.

Our son gambles: they said this to themselves at one point, even though I was in the house. And here their words are accurate. The disease. The vice. The gambling. E' zúg – the game.

We climb into Lele's MiTo, a tight fit but Walter is good at wedging himself into the back seat. We turn on the radio and as we head down Via Marecchiese towards the hills I tell them about the Toscanello I found in his Adidas jacket. Walter recalls seeing him smoking one at his bistro: hunching over to inhale, the coal flaring with each pull.

I lay my head between the seat and the window – was that his position? I'm worrying my thumb with a fingernail.

'You're bleeding,' Walter tells me a bit later. Lele gives me a handkerchief and I wrap it around my finger. They still haven't revealed our secret destination.

He repeats it ad infinitum: at Tre Stelle I tripped over this heel here, stiff as a mule's hoof. And bends down to slap it with his palm.

It's chilly but it's the chill of the Marecchia Valley that takes a while to enter your bones. We park and walk towards the stellario, a group of flat stone slabs crowning the gentle ridge.

On the way we buy three beers at a little grocery shop and carry them in the bag, then we clamber up the path. Walter knows the way, which means we're screwed for sure, and in fact he leads us astray; we wander this way and that, and before we arrive the beers are gone.

We lie down with our jackets under our backs, and the sun still has something of early autumn about it. I put an arm over my face, perhaps doze off, and when I lift it they're smoking.

'You know what we think?' Lele says. 'That you're free now.'

The blessing one of us would intone, in Milan, before opening a new deck: 'I did what I had to do, I was what I wanted to be.'

He left me eighteen thousand euros in cash and a plot of undevelopable land in San Zaccaria valued at nine thousand euros, plus properties in Rimini and Montescudo. Lorenzi the notary informed me of this on the phone during his condolence call. There's also an envelope, though Lorenzi doesn't know what's inside. He'll give it to me when I go by the offices to sign the paperwork.

'And when will you go and sign?' Walter asks.

'Monday.'

We're waiting for dusk, convinced there will be shooting stars in Pennabilli, even in November.

Walter pulls himself up. 'What do you think is in the envelope?'

'Instructions for the Montescudo place. Or debts.'

'Bar America?'

'Maybe.'

'He never said anything to you?'

'Just that they'd paid it off with part of my mother's severance money.'

'Then it must be Montescudo.'

'Or,' Lele says excitedly, 'maybe it'll be something about farmland. Like: never sell until it becomes developable.'

Walter lies back down. 'Or about pussy: don't get married, hold the course, don't let Bibi and the others take you for a ride.'

'He's next,' I say, pointing to Lele.

He flips me the sign of the horns. 'You're the one who should watch out: after a burial there's always a baby.'

An hour after he died, I called Bibi. Do you want to see him before they take him away? I was scared and she heard it and didn't reply. She said only, my love.

When I hung up I pictured her coming over and sitting right next to the bed. Him with the sheet up to his neck. The smell of aftershave and of putrefaction and his green face. I felt a kind of vertigo, as if I had actually allowed him to be defiled.

Walter and Lele and I huddle together. We're all sitting on a single stellario slab. They put me in the middle, it's cold, and Walter decides to get porchetta sandwiches down at the little grocery shop while we wait for the autumn meteors, which are worth double.

'Double what?'

'Double wishes.'

'And what do you want double of?'

'Another location. By the beach – fish and chips. Twice the income.'

We don't see any meteors and Lele shows us Ursa Major and Taurus and Walter eats half of my porchetta too. We drink chinotto and burp quietly and then burp with moon-shaped mouths puffing clouds of breath into the cold night. I want to go home but they won't let me. So I tell them how in recent times he'd been going dancing at the Atlantide, the arthouse cinema in Piazza Tripoli.

'Oh.' Lele pulls himself up from the stone. 'They have dancing?'

'In summer. That was his haunt at night there towards the end.'

'You followed him?' Walter doesn't wait for an answer. 'You did well, just tell people he was going catfishing at the quarry pond.'

'The fuck do catfish have to do with anything!' Lele snickers.

And we all snicker.

Then I start the game: 'A million euros richer and twenty years younger.' The words catch in my throat.

They wait me out. Walter smokes and then says that he'd pay off his debts and buy that fish place by the sea, make it into a chain. Ça va sans dire.

Lele thinks it over. 'I'd use it to buy the quiet life. Put it in a new account and schedule a monthly transfer into the old one. For twenty years. Then I could raise a family because I'd have a steady income even if I got nowhere with auditions.'

'How large a transfer?'

'Three thousand, the twenty-seventh of every month.'

I pull out my phone to do the maths. 'Almost twenty-eight years of income.'

'The quiet life.'

The morning of his death, after the call to Bibi, I called Amedeo, who came at the end of his shift at the hospital. He entered the room, bent over the body.

Then he came over to me, took off his glasses, wiped them with the hem of his sweater, and pulled me to him with his gorilla arms.

I followed him into the kitchen, he leaned back against the cabinets.

'Nando suffered,' I said.

Amedeo started cleaning his glasses again.

I poured myself some water. 'I didn't have the guts to help him go. I never have the guts for shit.'

I'm shuddering from the cold. Lele squeezes in from my left and Walter from my right – they're freezing too. I suggest going home, they put up a fight but eventually we're agreed and head towards the car park. Walter offers to drive.

'I saw him die,' I say.

We take a couple of minutes to clear our throats. Lele goes first: 'I've never seen anyone die.' He's leaning forward from the back seat. 'Except my dog.'

'His chest was bloated.'

'Stop, please.' Walter turns the radio on and then off in a single gesture. He recounts how he'd find him at his bistro waiting off to one side until somebody noticed him. 'And if nobody happened to notice him, he'd just stand there puffing away by that little wall. One night I said to him, Nando, is that you? What're you hiding over there for? And he shrugged as if to say it's fine.'

'Did he ever have company?'

'Always. His cigarettes.'

He smoked and smoked and smoked.

After the Stumble he smokes in the morning and practises the hop every day, in the living room and bedroom. The whip of ankles, the friction of heel on carpet and rug, the gurgle of exertion audible down the hall. Twenty minutes, half an hour. He doesn't yet call it: e' sèlt-Scirea – the Scirea Hop.

'But this Scirea Hop thing. How'd it get lodged in your dad's brain like that?' The MiTo turns on to Via Magellano.

'Because of the Brescia–Juventus match from 1987. The snowstorm game. He found a photo of it at a market in Santarcangelo.'

'Hell of a player, Scirea.'

'But it wasn't just that. It was his bulldog face in that picture – spitting image of his father.'

Now Lele turns the radio on and then off. 'He showed it to me.'

'Scirea with his legs splayed between the opponent and the ball. He was flying like Carla Fracci.'

'The Scirea Hop. I saw him do it in Miramare.' Lele drums on the window. 'Good God what a thing.'

We pull in at the house and they offer to stay the night.

'Bibi's coming.'

'You sure?'

'I'm sure.'

They nod even though they always know when I'm lying. They let me out and drive off, the grumble of the MiTo fading down Via Magellano. I climb the steps in the dark, pass snaking boxes, the humming refrigerator, the ticking wall clock. The phosphorus-sulphide smell of matches on the air. The nun's-hat lamp: as a boy I was terrified I'd leave it on and would go back to double check before he had a chance to notice.

I lift my hand to the switch and press it. The bulb blazes. I go to the dining room, lift my hand to the switch, and press. I go to the bathroom, press. And the stairwell, and the kitchenette, and my bedroom; I light up the other bathroom, the study, the box room; I turn on bedside lamps, the television, the lamp on the table and on the trumeau cabinet, the floor lamp in the living room; I illuminate the sink, the oven, the range hood; I turn on the two emergency lights in the hallway. The house, Via Magellano, Rimini, and this singular dazzlement.

I am free: an orphan. I am an orphan: free. I approach his room and see again his dangling leg tapping against the nights.

One afternoon – he was already very sick – as I was adjusting the pillows at his side: 'That ten thousand four hundred you weren't paid.' He broke off.

'It was the truth.'

'Really?'

'They really owed me.'

His eyes closed.

'And you, Nando. My bag and the briscola.'

They opened wide. 'Me what?'

'When I got here from Milan for your birthday. My bag was opened. And when you wanted to play cards, after dinner.'

'The open bag's a figment.'

'You didn't open it.'

'Nope.'

'What about the briscola after dinner?'

'Well.'

'You wanted to know if I'd started again.'

He slipped an extra pillow out and nodded. 'Seeing if you were my boy or that other one.'

'And what did you find out?'

'My boy.'

One boy or the other. A phrase he used with her too when he'd put her up to calling me in Milan to see how I was. As soon as the call was over he'd ask her: ours or that other one – the zúgadör? The gambler.

And one evening, at dinner. Without looking up from his plate he grunts that the only thing better than Tre Stelle is the Grand Gala at Gabicce.

'Then you guys should enter it and stop talking about it,'
I blurt.

'It's not like it's for stumblers, the Gala.'

I leave the house at half past one. The intersection of Via Magellano and Via Mengoni is lit by a cone of street-light and the cold has silvered the pavement. Exactly where Walter and Lele left me after Pennabilli. Being held at bay by them. And by Bibi, Don Paolo, by the dead, by Romagna. The sky is slate and streaked with ragged clouds and winter is ready.

I take the Renault 5. I open the throttle and the muffler calms down. I leave Ina Casa behind, I head towards the Padulli neighbourhood, slow down in front of an apartment complex under construction. The condo with the big oleander is just past the building site. Lights are on above, the ground floor is dark. I pull over where she pulled over the night she followed me, and I look through the gate: I don't see Bruni's Audi – I no longer recognise any of the cars.

I swat the bracelet hanging from the rearview. The check blanket is on the back seat, the ashtray is still clean, and under the seat is the small cushion I used to put between his side and the door. I take it out, wedge it between my knees and squeeze. I open my legs, squeeze. I drive off.

The Renault 5 shrieks through the first thirty metres and then becomes the Milva of Rimini with its contralto rumble. I park in front of the house and walk down Via Magellano, breath turning to steam and extending beyond my nose. I take the cobblestoned path that goes by the primary school: an alley of cats, three of which crouch along its edges. One – grey with a blotch at the base of its tail – rises as I pass and follows me to Largo Bordoni. The narrow piazza is empty, I sit on the bench. Beyond this housing complex is the church: all those people who came to the funeral.

Vendor of newspapers, assistant lifeguard, bartender, clerk in a clothes shop, copywriter, gambler, creative director in an advertising agency, creative consultant, gambler still.

They said: he's passed. They said: he's gone. They said: he's no longer with us.

Before the coffin is loaded into the hearse, Giulia looks at me from across the room and I look back. She doesn't come over; her hair is past her shoulders. She would have said: he's dead. Nando Pagliarani is dead. Your dad is dead.

And that June, on Via Meravigli in Milan, a timed game. Meet at six, start at a quarter past, finish at nine. In timed games you play for the whole prearranged duration. No delays, no backing out after you've said yes. One hand follows another until the time expires. The trick is to guess whether, when the time is almost up, you'll be able to finish the current hand and start a final one in which you can try either to recoup losses or consolidate winnings: the farewell hand.

By 8.20 I was down six thousand six hundred. I calculated that we'd be able to get two more hands in before nine. Instead, the next hand dragged on for so long that it was going to be the farewell hand. I had a pair of tens. There were three of us left, including a long player. Long players are players who slow things down to foil other players' attempts to salvage their evenings at the buzzer. Usually they're the ones who have done well up to that point.

At quarter to nine we were still at the table – which meant no hope of another hand, though if necessary we could go beyond the ending time to properly conclude the current hand. At that stage the pot grows more freely than usual, since the window for digging out of holes or waiting for better luck is about to close for the evening. And this is where gamblers *tilt*. Tilting: tapping into the power of extreme recklessness and daring.

At ten past nine the pot was at thirty-eight hundred. By twelve past we had shown our cards: a bluff by the long player, two pair for the other guy. I had lost another five thousand and change. About twelve thousand in total, with only four thousand cash in hand. IOUs for the rest.

After leaving the apartment I remember hearing a commotion in the little piazza off Via delle Orsole: a cluster of people celebrating, summer holidays imminent, and behind them that fresco of the Madonna and Child uncovered four centuries ago by a worker cleaning the wall with an apron. I went up to it, stood in front of it, examined Mary and the Christ child, her cerulean robe and his dove-grey skin, and I felt the need to sit down, to stretch my arms and my back, and to feel my plundered pockets – cheque gone, cash gone. I stood back up and crossed the little square again, and as I was about to leave it, passing the last few souls, seven years after my first game, I could feel what it was: not the thrill; not the hit of adrenaline; not the secrecy or the pawing after possible riches; not the compensation or the rush of risk; not the tilt or the stirred blood. Coming out of the little square, a phrase I once heard a guy say – months earlier in Novara, at the end of a furious hand – finally made sense to me: We're dense tonight, eh.

We're dense tonight. We've concentrated as much life as we can into the least possible time. Denseness. The Madonna and the haloed Christ, the blessèd in one corner of Milan. We and our as-much-life-as-we-can: the blessèd in one corner of Milan. The blessèd and the blessèd.

Don Paolo, during the eulogy: Nando, the man whose feet were always ready for a party.

On Monday Bibi accompanies me to the notary's office. We wait in the waiting room. As soon as we're called she tells me she's not coming in. She's sitting crookedly, squeezing her hands together and biting her bottom lip.

Lorenzi's office smells like paint. I take a seat in a brown leather chair with rounded arms, accept condolences again. The secretary opens a folder and hands the notary some papers: eighteen thousand two hundred and twenty euros in the bank account, the property in Rimini, the property in Montescudo, the Renault 5, and an undevelopable piece of land in San Zaccaria.

Then they hand me the envelope: it bears his initials and, on the back, a date from four months ago. They give me a letter opener, I rip it open, and inside I find a printed page signed Ferdinando Pagliarani.

It's an investment plan, arranged with the bank, that I can follow if I want. According to regulations I'll have to be briefed directly by the relevant branch.

I grimace.

'Everything all right?' Lorenzi asks.

'It's not debts.'

He stops practising the hop over and over in the living room and garage. Never another word about the Stumble. Never another word about the Gala in Gabicce. Never again a real dance.

Summer ends, and when the first Saturday night of their off-season rolls around, I find them lounging in the living room.

'What's up?'

'We've had enough.'

When we leave the notary I reveal to Bibi that the envelope contained an investment plan. She doesn't know what to say, finally murmuring: 'He knew who he was dealing with.'

I look at her.

'You were a big spender, right?'

'Not exactly.'

'No?'

'You must've heard that from Daniele.'

She rubs my shoulders. 'C'mon, I was joking.'

'Then this big spender will take you for a dinner out tonight.' The phrase *dinner out* gets mangled in my throat. I stop walking.

'Hey.' She takes my wrist.

'I told him neither of us cooks and you should've seen his face.'

'What was it like?'

'*Heaven forbid.*'

Bibi smiles, a comma at each corner of her mouth. She takes a big stride and pulls me along. 'Nando was always cooking and tonight we'll be served and fawned over. Tagliatelle.'

'Tagliatelle?'

'And envelopes with investment plans.' She pulls me through Piazza Cavour and through the pedestrian zone to the right of Teatro Galli, me and my grudge: against him, against foresight, against a life of saving.

Bruni's number. I have a vague memory of tearing the page out of my old Moleskine and slipping it into a book. I riffle through the volumes on the floating shelves in my room and in the big built-ins. I take out a book, riffle through it, drop it, take, riffle, drop. A heap grows on the floor. I walk over it out of the room, check my phone again. Nothing. A thorough purge, after my promise to quit on the day of her funeral.

The brother of an old high school friend might have it. He showed up one night at the oleander condo. Of all of them, he's the only one I know how to track down.

I call, he asks no questions, but he'll have to look for it in turn. We talk about his sister: she became a statistician at FAO in Rome. We talk about Nando: he heard from his mother that I lost him and offers his condolences. Ten minutes after we hang up he texts me Bruni's number.

Farewell to dance. On Saturday nights she paints down in the laundry room, he watches war films and eats licorice wheels.

At a restaurant in nearby Canonica, Bibi and I actually do order tagliatelle. And red wine, and local guinea fowl, and piada with vegetables au gratin. To finish, an Albana Dolce and slices of ciambella on a tray. Bibi inspects them: the slice with the most powdered sugar, the thickest slice, the crusty end piece. She moves her nose over each, then pours the Albana into the two glasses, hands one to me, and snatches up the end piece. She lifts it over her Albana and dunks it in. She pinches off the soaked tip and puts it in her mouth, eyeing me seriously, then dunks it again and puts it to her lips to suck the sweetness out. She nibbles, drips, wipes, still serious. She sees the sludge at the bottom of her glass and takes her spoon and scoops it up, it's good, and brings it to her mouth and closes her eyes.

'Oh, sorry,' she says, almost laughing, when she reopens them.

And in her the last part of him: he who had heard about her, he who was there when she and I began. If she didn't contain him, would she be her?

Three conditions for remaining in the organisation. Condition one: have references. Condition two: honour your IOUs. Condition three: never cheat.

Outside the restaurant is that Romagna dark that swallows even the moon. We're parked at the far end of the gravel lot. Bibi turns on her phone light and tells me she's working on the *Regimbartia* beetle: the only insect to be excreted alive after passing through a frog's digestive system. It doesn't die; it windmills its legs to rush through the stomach and out before the gastric juices can dissolve it.

'Thanks for killing my coffee buzz, Beatrice Giacometti.'

She waves her mobile phone and turns it off, and we sink back into the dark of Romagna. Nothing left but the crunch of gravel, then not even that. I turn around, stand still, take a step back. Bibi, where are you, Bibi?

Out of nowhere she throws her arms around me.

He used to call me in Milan once a week with that May-I? voice. How're things how're things. If I called it was because I had some news, or because I had just resurfaced. I'd pull out my phone and dial, putting on my nice voice.

And that day, two months after she had died, when I showed up in Rimini unannounced and he spotted me from the terrace, how're things how're things, half annoyed at being caught off guard. He opened the door for me, led the way up the stairs, kept me at the entry to the kitchen, from where I could glimpse the LPs piled on the table, amid peanut shells and a can of sweetcorn. The office chair instead of dining chairs, copper pans in the sink, the record player on the dresser. The smell of old soup and flies swirling around.

'Yesterday the music inventory began.' He opened the fridge and rummaged around inside. 'Did you know I didn't do the shopping, Sandrin?'

'Tell me how you're doing.'

'I'm doing well.'

'Me too.'

He took out the Emmental and cut me a piece. 'There are crackers.'

I found a corner of the table, took a bite of Emmental. He stood there motionless and watched me chew between Stevie Wonder and Ivan Graziani.

I can't sleep. I get up, go to the kitchen, read his investment proposal. His sorrowful signature, the tail of the o. I leave the papers on the table: I don't know what to do with the pans he used to make his retirement recipe. Or the canning jars. The collection of spice containers. The nuts in the straw basket. Our briscola deck, tied with a green rubber band. I pick it up. It's cold in my fist. I squeeze it and feel the whisper of a tingle in my fingertips, of pressure on my sternum, feel him in front of me, smoke from his cigarette trailing gently away.

After they have stopped dancing, a month and a half after the Stumble, I find him in the study with the Scirea photo in his hand.

'Come here, Sandro.' He turns on the table lamp. 'Look how easy he stays up. A push at the right moment.'

His arms rising as he lay dying, the repeated thud of his hands on the mattress. His face scraping the headboard. His twisted neck straightening. His new face: mouth open, upper lip split.

They really hadn't danced again. But he did put the Scirea picture in his wallet. And he had reorganised the LPs in the living room, though he hadn't put any of them on the record player since Tre Stelle.

Then on a certain afternoon: the blinds halfway down, the Bee Gees on, and the thud of feet trying the hop again.

On the phone Bruni is surprised and friendly. He has been out of the big organisation for some time, but he can still scare up a game on short notice. I ask how he knows I want a game. He laughs his laugh, halfway between a girl's squeal and a dry cough.

'I want to try again, yes.'

'How much?'

'Three thousand.'

'I'll call you in a couple of days.'

We celebrate the annual closing of Walter's bistro as if he were the one going dark. Each autumn he goes into hibernation: doesn't travel anywhere exotic, just barricades himself in his home in the village of San Giovanni and cooks, emerging only on Sundays for lunch at seafood places, a few trips to the countryside. Then at Easter he rolls up the blinds and starts again.

During the toasts, his name comes up: to Nando. It's Lele who says it, and Bibi tops up my glass. We're all there, on the veranda overlooking the canal. Tables are stacked in the back, the Gradella sign is wrapped in cellophane, Rimini's sparkle fading. And Milan's, which vanished with Nando.

After Giulia, they used to ask if there was anyone I had a fondness for. She would say *fondness*, and his antennae would perk up to await my answer. Knowing I was in Milan, alone, in a two-room apartment with a rickety table. Milan and its concrete that alters sons.

They came up, two months after Giulia left. They slept in the double bed and I took the sofa. In the morning I woke to the chirp of his screwdriver fixing my table: the glass top that reared up if you leaned your elbows on the edge.

'Do you snore?' Bibi asks.

'Do you?'

After the evening of Walter's closing, I invited her to spend the night at my place – a first.

When we got there I led the way downstairs. We crawled into bed: the mattress is comfortable, the air cold: I didn't have time to turn on the heat. The blankets come up to our noses.

'I snore a little.' She wedges her feet between my legs. We don't sleep, we do, we don't, then she does and I lie there beside her silhouette: the bony shoulder, the gentle hip. Any habit can be broken.

Then I fall asleep and when I wake up she's facing me, looking at me. And I look at her too, her sharp profile and crouched posture, her scent stretching across the pillow: and I see her. And: she's not a blur.

We go upstairs for breakfast. The kitchen has warmth, we close the door to keep it in. Bibi is standing, reaching towards the spices and preserves, touching them without moving them.

'Where did he sit?'

'Here,' I point to the chair near the stove.

'And what about you, Sandro?'

'Here,' and I point to the chair by the window. She takes my seat. I put the coffee on, lean back against the counter.

The Bee Gees, the Jackson Five, Chuck Berry. Every day he's showing signs of dancing in the house again, always by himself. Then she comes along and pulls out the shag record, the very one from the Stumble.

And she says: 'Let's give it another shot.'

I stop by the bank to deal with the will issue. They seat me in the manager's office. They offer condolences and inform me that he left specific instructions: he wants me to be fully informed about the investment plan in the notary's envelope before deciding whether to sign up or not. Or perhaps to find alternative plans.

I let them talk, it lasts about twenty minutes, I reply that I'll think about it. The manager talks some more about the pension fund and the hybrid emerging markets option. I ask for five thousand euros in cash.

Gambling cyclothymia: sine wave psychological motion, with six to eight emotional peaks on the day of a game. Emotional peaks: euphoria, palpitations and tremors, urgent limb movements, disperceptions. Emotional valleys: feeling anxious, uninterested in your surroundings, indifferent to others.

When I come out of the bank I hear my name: it's Patrizia from Sardinia. She waves an arm from the other side of Via Marecchiese and makes her way towards me. She has a bakery sack sticking out of her bag.

'Sandro' – she's adjusting her knitted cap – 'I saw you go in, do you have time for coffee?'

Your dad and I used to go to the cinema once a month, on Wednesday nights. Occasionally dinner too. He'd ask me about your mum, how I knew things about her that he'd never heard: I even told him about that day we rented a canoe in Riccione and the current swept us out to sea. You should have seen him: canoe, what canoe? Current, what current? Caterina never told me that. So many questions. Sometimes we just walked. And no, he never asked me to go dancing.

Patrizia gives me a ride home. We park in front of the gate, engine running, and as I'm about to get out she asks if she can say goodbye to the house. She walks through the gate, but not to the door. She looks up at the bedroom window, goes around the courtyard and over to the garden.

It's barren, the earth pale with frost, and she harries a clump of dirt with the toe of her shoe.

What not to do when you take a seat: keep a tally of potential debt as you play. Of how much you could afford to lose. And of what you're up against. Think about financial consequences, about your actual ability to repay debts, about the repercussions on your private life.

In the beginning, when you're still the new guy, they limit you: you can get only as many chips as you have cash for, no more. Loans are never granted. Later, they might be: loans, IOUs. In time the organisation learns how each person handles their wallet and excludes them from tables beyond their means, or from new hands where further bleeding could leave creditors exposed. The final stage is when you're given free rein for anything.

One strategy that worked: before going through the front door, write down realistic limits and consequences. Write them down, but don't think about them.

I inform Amedeo that he left a smock here. Also some syringes, medicines and other items he may need. He says he was already planning to drop by, and might we have lunch today? He adds that it would mean a lot to him to come to the house.

He arrives before one: he gets out of his Toyota and opens the back door, extracting a little girl, and they come slowly up the steps. We hug in the hall, the little girl scrunching in to let us, and when I pull away she straightens out again: she has her father's blazing eyes. She reaches a finger out to touch my mouth, my teeth. Then she is curious about the boxes, leaning down as if to grab one.

'This little girl is Margherita and she's very thirsty.' Amedeo brings her close to me and she tugs at my beard, stretches her lips into a duck's beak.

I take her hand even though she is clinging to her father. We all go into the kitchen, he sets her down on the table, and I expect a baby bottle. Amedeo signals to me that a cup is fine. I fill one and sit and help her hold it as she drinks.

'The night your dad and I watched *Fight Club*, remember that?'

But it's all a jumble to me. Nights, mornings.

Amedeo helps me clear the table. 'At one point he was in a lot of pain and wanted morphine. I went to get it for him and when I came back with it he asked if I would help him die.'

I'm washing the dishes, drops of grease are floating in the pan. We had cod and cayenne potatoes. Margherita is crawling down the hall, Amedeo is keeping an eye on her. 'I never have the guts for shit either, Sandro.'

The little girl has reached the living room and is playing with a velvet cushion. 'Papà!' She flitters her arms.

I go. She's puzzled, looks for her father, but as soon as I give her another cushion she presses her cheek against it.

Amedeo joins us. 'But what if it's not about guts. What if it's fear of God.'

The two of them are in the garage, taking apart the rollbox over the window because the shutter is stuck. 'We can't go to Tre Stelle again, Caterina.'

She's holding the ladder and is about to say fine, they won't go anymore. Instead she gives his ankles a squeeze: 'Let's try Gabicce, Nando, the Grand Gala.'

He twists around and looks down at her from that height.

Before leaving, Amedeo shows me a comfortable mode for holding babies. *Comfortable mode*, he says, adjusting his glasses. He bends down, lifts Margherita up, and wedges her horizontally under one arm like a rugby ball, then walks down the hall. She doesn't protest; she just adapts and dangles from her daddy's arm.

'You try.'

'With me she'll cry.'

'Try it.'

I try it. It's funny having her there, her legs and arms and floppy little head. The sly expression scrutinising me as we walk past the bedrooms and back into the living area. Margherita and I in comfortable mode, travelling through the house of empty wardrobes. Then I pull her up and there she is. I kiss the back of her head and hand her to her father.

An hour after Margherita and Amedeo have left, Bruni calls. He tells me there's a sit-and-go game with a six thousand buy-in. Down in Viserba.

'Six thousand, no. Three at the most, plus your cut.'

'You've got timid.'

'Three at the most.'

'I'll ask.'

'Thanks.'

He'll let me know by this evening. When I hang up I hold my arms out – a faint trembling.

The other indicator is tactile. I pull out the five thousand I withdrew from the bank and add it to the one thousand six hundred and fifty from the safe. I take them to the kitchen. I slip off the band and flip through the notes. Their graininess on my thumb, the knurling of the paper against the side of my fingers, the nicked corners. The hundreds robust. The twenties nimble. The fifties worn. At one time my skin conductance would rise in less than ten seconds: sweat gleaming on my fingertips, skin thickening.

My way of counting cash: eyelids low, I clamp the stack between the middle and ring fingers of my left hand and fold it forward, fanning it slightly with a push of my left thumb and pulling each note back with my right index, push and pull, neck pulsing just below the Adam's apple. I pause, start over, until the fibres of the paper are warm.

Even as a child: my grandmother gives me two hundred thousand lire for communion, in an envelope with a card. I take them out, heart fluttering, certain I'll be able to have more, able to have it all.

He used to beat himself up because the place was empty. Bar America. Friends would come by and find him, her, one customer, and me doing homework in the corner.

How do we bring people in: the refrain of those twenty-six months. Then she started holding a painting class there, on Tuesday nights. Then jazz, on Friday nights. Then coffee and a pastry for two thousand lire. Then they started pulling down the shutter before dinner.

By mid-afternoon Bruni still hasn't called. I start prepping the lectures for my university course, move jars of preserves from the pantry to the dresser, empty the sideboard of pots and pans, arrange them in the cupboards. I climb the step-ladder and clean the window panes – from up here you can see a piece of the Sabatinis' yard. They've started getting it ready for their Christmas lights, which they always put up a month and a half in advance. By now he would have thrown open the window to greet them, letting all that cold whip into the house.

I visit him, throwing away the old flowers and the Railway Social wreath. The photo of him laughing in the bar in Cervia: his San Zaccaria relatives chose it.

Towards evening Lele drops by unannounced: he has been cast for ten scenes in a series about Monica Vitti. Walter also shows up and we open beers and the kitchen fills with smoke and they sit now on the table, now on the counter. Lele is an animal lover and checks the windowsill, points out the lack of breadcrumbs. I show him the foil-wrapped package on the microwave; he opens it and finds half an almond cake, which he crumbles and scatters on the outer sill. 'When robins appear, success is near.'

'Proclaims the clairvoyant ornithologist.' Walter shuts the window because he's cold.

'Caterina used to think so too,' I say.

'That Lele's a clairvoyant ornithologist?'

'That robins bring luck.'

Walter raises his glass of beer: 'To robins and to Caterina and to the clairvoyant ornithologist. And to Monica Vitti!'

'You and your toasts.' We all raise our glasses.

The Grand Gala at the Baia Imperiale in Gabicce: thirty professional couples and twenty amateur couples. She calls the organiser and learns that registration has closed. She doesn't insist; she's no good at that on the phone.

Bruni tries to reach me when Lele and Walter are still here. I let the phone vibrate, get up and go into my room, tell him I'll call him back soon. When I return Lele's in the hallway, Walter's in the kitchen emptying the bowl of peanuts into his palm and dumping them into his mouth. He points at me. 'We're moving to my place, since you've got fuck all in the fridge.'

'I'm knackered, guys.'

Meanwhile Lele slips down the hall towards the bed-rooms. He peeks in Nando's room, then returns and starts down the stairs. 'No dinner then? Is Bibi coming over?'

'Yeah, she is.'

On his way out he's giving me a look. Of relief? Of doubt? Of what?

She goes in person to the Baia Imperiale to sign them up for the Grand Gala.

The club is closed but the gate is open. She approaches and sees someone behind a glass door. She pauses, not feeling up to begging. Then she spots the photos of dancers on the walls.

Apart from dancing, he was never a very physical man. Except: what about when he was smearing his face with Saint Honoré cake? Or rubbing sandpaper over wood? Or carrying thirty-kilo stones to carve? And what about the table edge he'd grip in July and August as we ate: hand on the cool wood as a refuge from the muggy air. He was always sweaty and you couldn't brush against him. And that one time I saw him naked: I must have been ten, playing football at Marecchia Park, the ball got punctured, and I ran home to get the spare, taking the steps two at a time and dashing past their bedroom on the way to mine, barely turning my head – and him there, hair wet, bathrobe on the chair, his hands by his knees clutching the sides of the underpants he was about to pull up. His cock dangling, large, swinging in the air.

I do call Bruni back: he has found a sit-and-go game in Covignano, near Bar Ilde, he'll confirm it in a few minutes.

Four thousand, or perhaps less. Good people, he'll vouch for me. Six players.

'I want to play a round.'

'A round, two.'

'A round or two.'

'All right, I'll let them know.'

'Thanks.'

'Sandro?'

'Yeah.'

'You disappeared.'

I switch the phone to my other ear. 'I'm back now.'

He says nothing, clicks the roof of his mouth. He won't be there, doesn't come in person anymore. The appointment is for nine – he gives me the address and phone number.

I slide my phone into my pocket, lean back against the counter. After Walter and Lele the kitchen table is askew, three chairs scattered around it, our jumble on top of it: peanut bowl, crisps, licorice, two lighters. Walter tried to fold the empty Marlboro pack into a plane but ended up with a winged tank. I advance it over the wood; it takes off and turns into a fighter-bomber. It flies through the kitchen, past counters and shelves, and lands by the wicker basket. I leave it there, grab the briscola deck, take the rubber band off and squeeze it in my right hand.

'Will it be a lucky night,' I ask aloud, shuffling as she insisted before reading the cards, slowly, staring at some fixed point in front of her. A slip of paper falls out of the deck, folded in quarters. I open it. His handwriting: *Amaracmànd, Sandrin* – I beg of you, Sandro.

My box of cardinal peaches: a 2011 game in the Miramare neighbourhood, on the day of the Notte Rosa – the first of July. A mob of kids was partying below the apartment where we were going to play.

Bruni had been given a big game and trusted it. Eight thousand buy-in: I emptied my bank account and was twenty-nine hundred short. I asked Walter for two hundred with some excuse and borrowed four from a guy in Misano. For the remaining twenty-three hundred I made some phone calls to Milan – nothing. I thought of selling the bracelet I got for my eighteenth birthday or asking some Rimini players, but I didn't want to let it be known I was short. That left them: my mother kept her debit card in a drawer in the study. I allowed myself two withdrawals on the eve of the day of the game, one before midnight and one after, and I took the rest from the safe. I didn't think about what I would tell her, or tell him, as soon as they found out. You never think about that.

There were five of us, all strangers, brought together by Bruni from as far as Viareggio to eliminate any edge from knowing other players. A 'no-exit' game, which meant three rounds, no time limit and no additional hands. In such a scenario there's no dropping out before the predetermined number of games have been played. IOUs are granted, precisely to allow the three acts to be completed even if someone runs out of chips while a game is in progress. If you're down after the first or second round, you have to leave that disappointment behind as you enter the third. Clean slate. If you're up after the first or second, same thing. If you're more or less level after the first two, you enter the third with a clear head.

For most of us, the first round sets the tone for the evening: a disastrous opener can cast a daunting pall on the second and then third rounds. A chain of events leading to poorly executed bluffs, telling physicality, declining self-control: lost houses, transferred car titles, exposed assets, self-inflicted wounds. Like Giannini in Milan who began a third round down twenty-seven thousand and ended up signing away his house in Santa Margherita to a guy from Monte Carlo. Or the opposite: a progressively amassed fortune and a memorable night. According to rumour, that's how Filoni came by the Hotel Bussler in Rome in 2002.

Given Bruni's eight thousand buy-in, one could potentially be in the hole as much as sixty thousand by the end of the night. Hardly anyone has the cash to cover such losses, which is why everyone always has guarantors present at a no-exit game – people who would handle any bother over the following weeks, having made sure in advance that none of us would cause problems. For me there was Bruni himself, who in return would receive a quarter of my potential winnings.

Bruni was sitting on a sofa in the next room: he was the one who had brought the new deck. After the first round I was down three thousand. After the second, nine thousand something. They had a sheet of paper to keep track of our gains and losses relative to our initial buy-ins. At the start of the third round, two players were in deeper holes than me: the guy from Correggio was down about twenty thousand, the guy from Piacenza about sixteen thousand.

From the window we could hear the kids partying: that Rimini, that version of me I already no longer remember:

the laughter, the techno on the beach, no thought but to have a good time. I told myself that having lost in the first round, having lost in the second, I wanted to lose in the third as well. I wanted to lose it all, finish with a debt so hard to set right it would force me to seek help from home, the bank, friends, marking me as irreversibly damaged, allowing me perhaps to get back out there, with the kids, the music on the beach, dancing and drinking and chasing youth.

While I waited for my cards, I planted my elbows on the arms of the chair and lowered my head: I wasn't going to try to bluff, I was just going to replace my weak cards and play whatever I had in my hand. I was thirty-two years old, I was living well in Milan, I could have been married, I was respected in the advertising business.

Instead, I was dealt trip sevens. Being dealt a hand like that always feels amazing, even to veterans. Without moving my elbows from the armrests, I checked and saw the seven of clubs, the seven of spades, the seven of hearts. I banished my disbelief, telling myself it had happened: I had been dealt three of a kind – a 2.11 per cent chance.

I bet, drew two cards, but the new ones changed nothing. After five raises, I asked to borrow another nine thousand. Bruni agreed. We played until there was thirty-nine thousand in the pot. Then we showed and the pot was mine.

They noted each person's balance on the sheet of paper: they settled my accounts, deducting from my winnings the losses of the first two rounds, minus the buy-in. They gave me two cheques and eleven thousand in cash. We rose from the table; those who had lost left immediately. I waited, looked at the table, the dirty ashtrays and sweet wrappers, the cigar butt. Then I went over to the window again. And all this was there below me: the beachfront, the music, the Notte Rosa kids who on that first night of July were carrying away the Sandro I would never be again.

Amaracmànd, Sandrin – I beg of you, Sandro. I leave his note beside the briscola deck on the counter where he used to slice vegetables. I wash the peanut bowl and put it back in the sideboard, throw out the crisps, throw out the cigarette butts and empty beer bottles. I wipe the table, dry it, straighten the chairs. Walter left his phone charger plugged in by the microwave – I set it aside. I open the window, the sill is strewn with almond-cake crumbs. It's never too early for robins.

I beg of you, Sandro.

But the cards have said: tonight you will win.

Caterina and Nando Pagliarani, Grand Gala 2009, Baia Imperiale, Gabicce. Registration category: amateur. Check-in at 7.30 p.m.

Day games. In Milan, in spring, to sit at a table when it's still light out, to get up when restaurants are still open and the air retains some industriousness. People walking by, ties loosened, blazers folded over forearms after leaving offices, passing young people drinking at outdoor tables. It's important to know you have to go back home, to force yourself to stick to a time – an urgency that limits the risk of haemorrhage. And once home to say: I worked late at the office.

Never to play at night in Milan. The strange stillness, the way everything seems reparable.

In Gabicce, the night of the Grand Gala, the garbino is blowing in from the Adriatic. As they approach the club he slows down. She smooths one of his lapels and takes him by the arm.

The diamond-shaped lights on the dance floor: they always talked about those diamond-shaped lights.

Bruni calls me again because he needs to tell me who's running the game tonight: a lawyer from Ferrara who has lived in Zurich for twenty years. He's from the Venice organisation. A separate group that won't tolerate delays or lack of cash.

'Okay.'

'You're vouched for and that's enough for him.'

'The other players?'

'The Cardigan from Bologna – remember him?'

'Yeah.'

'He's the only one you know. The rest are reliable people from other places.'

In the early days I showed up for games at the last minute. Then that evening on Corso Garibaldi I came to the neighbourhood an hour early: I wandered around the address, drank an amaro at Tombon, and walked up and down Via Moscova – the Milan of buried canals and trepidation, crooked alleys and solemn boulevards. I came back to the address, smoked, walked away. I returned at the appointed time.

All that back and forth meant I was worn out at the table: fatigue made me almost apathetic, unflappable, inscrutable. I won thirteen hundred euros. From then on I always showed up early.

It's two hours until Bruni's game in Covignano. I preempt Bibi's phone call and she gets right to it: she doesn't feel like going to the cinema with her friends, so why don't I drop by her house for a molecular exchange – no one will be the wiser. I tell her I feel like being alone. We're both quiet, then she wishes me a good evening, her voice still beautiful, and I too could say: my love.

An hour and a half later in the car I think of her again, her serious way of saying *molecular exchange*. And again as I park at Bar Ilde, and as I walk back towards the game, and Bibi again in the moment before the game begins, at which point certainties surrender to possibilities.

The Baia Imperiale had a narrow dance floor and you had to be careful. They would be the sixth pair to dance. One pair at a time, the others all standing except the jury, who are already seated to await the professionals.

She got into position first. Then he planted his heels and whispered to his left foot: *fà e' brèv* – be good.

If someone seemed off to him, he'd say they danced badly. With anyone, the slightest sign was enough for him to pass judgement: *l è sgrazièd* – he's a klutz.

'How can you tell?' she used to ask.
'I can tell.'
'From what? The face, the voice? The way of moving?'
'Can't you see it?'
'No, I can't.'

Then, as soon as he was proved right, he felt sorry.

'What about me?' she prompted.

'What about you, Caterina?'

'Do I dance badly or well?'

'You dance well.'

'What about me?' I asked.

'You're clever.'

I check the address Bruni gave me: the house is on a lane that rises towards a circular street whose dwellings squat behind vegetation. It's a marlstone villa with three chimneys, palm trees in the garden and wisteria that canopies the veranda. The blinds are raised except on the ground floor. I'm eighteen minutes early.

I light a cigarette, take a drag, and two headlights flash from across the street. They're coming from a car parked at an angle: it's Lele's MiTo. I walk away; he gets out and follows.

He comes up behind me. 'You don't have to stay here.'

'Who did you talk to.'

'Guess.'

'You called Bruni?'

'I knew you weren't with Bibi because she's at the cinema with the others.'

'Mind your own fucking business.'

'You don't have to stay here.'

I scrape a shoe on the ground. 'Mind your own fucking business.'

'You already know you can do it.' He takes hold of my arm.

I yank it away. 'Get lost.'

'You can do it.' He takes my arm again. I pull it loose and walk away, back to Bar Ilde, to my car, and I drive up to the San Fortunato church. I pull over at the viewpoint. The MiTo arrives and parks, and Lele gets out and taps on my window: 'Do what you have to. I'll wait for you here.'

Three-fourths of the way through the shag at the Grand Gala he altered his position – no one watching noticed. But she did, when she lost sight of him. The Pasadèl and his step-back: the secret space for the Scirea Hop. The risk of a lifetime.

Lele really does stay at the viewpoint. I return to the villa of the three chimneys and wait for stillness. It comes fast, as it always does so near a table: the rest fades. I call the number Bruni gave me. A weak voice answers. I say my name and the voice says he'll come let me in.

A man in his seventies approaches the gate, invites me to enter, leads the way. He's wearing thick-frame glasses and a shirt that's buttoned to the top. He steps aside to make room for me: 'Welcome.'

The living room is to the right. We'll play on a round table in front of one of the windows with lowered blinds. The light comes from lamps on the shelves and on a chest of drawers, on a TV stand with no TV. One lamp is on the floor. The other players are over in the corner, serving themselves from the bar cart. I say hello, a young man in a baseball cap reciprocates, he must be in his thirties. I nod to the guy who lived in Bologna in the days of the oleander condo: he's glad to see I haven't changed; he hasn't either, with that cardigan he'll take off mid-round.

The sofa has been moved against the windows on the other side of the room, which is furnished with empty shelves and a little table with a crystal curio in the shape of a polar bear. The stale smell is recent and the house has a lived-in feel: as if the occupants had vacated in a hurry, accomplishing a prudent relocation. I sit on the arm of the sofa, the others drift apart, and we wait for the two who are missing. Waiting is fine, though there's an unspoken limit: twenty minutes. Beyond that, any player can ask to start, cutting the late players out, or else can leave, excused by all. This time the latecomers arrive after fifteen minutes: they're together and look like brothers to me, with the same humped nose. One smiles: I can tell it's a nervous grin because he keeps it.

No one asks for anything; everyone is vouched for by someone, except the septuagenarian, who instead opens a portfolio to show us his cash. We've all been vetted by a non-player, who is also vouched for: it was always Bruni who did this before, holding each player's buy-in separately and keeping an eye on those who, with the table's approval, go beyond their wallets and take on IOUs. It has happened to me twice: they set up repayment schedules, which are usually soft. They also require that there be someone else who knows the losing player and agrees to settle for him, if need be. I've used Bruni himself and my CEO in Milan. They almost never ask for interest. If you fail to pay your debt, make it right with people, you face expulsion from the organisation, and sometimes other kinds of reprisals.

The septuagenarian slips his portfolio into a leather briefcase: he undoes his top button and his neck ripples with a rich cough. He goes to the bar cart and pours himself a finger of vermouth; he could be a cushion, as they're called in Milan. A cushion is a pawn whose role in the game is to support one or more of the other players, fattening pots. But any of us could be, despite being vouched for.

I take off my coat, hang it on the coat rack and go over to the little table with the polar bear. I pick it up: against the light, the crystal's iridescence astonishes me. I hold it out and feel its weight. My fingertips are dry and my arm is steady, and when I bend it I don't feel any pressure rising to my neck. I go to the far side of the living room and peek through the open window: the parking area is now empty – the MiTo hasn't come back. I realise I still have the bear in my fist.

'Okay?' says the septuagenarian.

I return the bear to its place and we take our seats at the table. The chairs are comfortable and have armrests, which help: not having to support the weight of your arms fosters inertia, and inertia fosters the obfuscation of intent. Ideally you maintain a natural bearing throughout, but few can. Most will assert some physical tendency at the outset: perhaps they'll fidget noticeably, to cover any awkwardness when cards are in hand; or they'll make it obvious from the start that they have a restless arm, nothing to do with the cards, allowing themselves to channel tensions into that motion. One of the defences against carelessness remains the deflection: fixing your gaze on a specific spot on the table, the wall, a piece of furniture.

'Okay.' The septuagenarian finishes his vermouth and begins.

He rolls up his shirt sleeves and doles out the chips, converting our buy-ins into equal stacks. He proceeds carefully and at modest speed, has a thick wedding ring and a bracelet studded with small sailor knots. He opens the pack, tosses the wrapper to the floor and starts a riffle shuffle, palms pushing in to energise the motion and trigger the cascades that blend where they meet. A beating of wings. When he's satisfied, he has everyone stand: he hands us each a card. We turn them over: the high card is held by the brother with the grin, to whom the deck is passed. He's serious now, adjusting himself in his chair, ready to answer the call. He pushes a three-hundred-euro chip across the table, pressing it like a button as he releases it. He waits for us to do the same, we all do, so then he adds a second chip and starts to shuffle, and that thrumming hangs in the air when he's done. He passes the deck to his right for the cut, puts it back together. He deals, making sure we each get our card in a good spot, clockwise, card in a good spot, clockwise, card in a good spot. His eyes haven't left the pot, and then they do, to make sure we're all in order.

Getting your cards is a fork in the road: some players tend to anticipate that they'll be good before they see them, opening themselves to hard-to-hide disappointments. Others expect them to be weak, avoiding disappointed looks that could undermine a bluff. I'm in the latter camp, with a weakness for aces: having one gives me a thrill, even when it won't help me win. I don't know why, it just does.

The septuagenarian is the first to look at his cards: he lifts the corners and peeks, puts them down, peeks again –

it seems they must be good because he checks a third time as if for the pleasure of it. Or maybe they have potential but are jumbled, forcing someone with a poor memory to check them until they get a good handle on them. The others shift one edge over at a time, except for Bologna Cardigan, who has always had his own way of lifting the corners with his fingernails. The two brothers work identically: they lean down, shift one card from the next, fiddle with their chips. The guy in the baseball cap looks at his cards, rearranges them, seems laid back.

Each of them is the cards they hold. They're considering bluffs – foretaste of victory, prelude to defeat – or imagining lucrative interventions from the deck. This phase is called purgatory: it lasts forty seconds on average, longer if there is an alliance between some players and they want to start exhausting a fish. Extending purgatories can flush beginners out of their lairs. In 2014 we wore out one Genoa notary who tended to smooth his lapels when bluffing: he lost sixteen thousand in the fifth round, after we had worked him over in the purgatories of the first four.

Forty seconds pass and I'm the only one who hasn't looked at his cards. The septuagenarian is staring at me, my hands are resting on the table. My fingertips are lukewarm, my arms extended, my legs steady, my chest quiet.

The others are staring at me too.

The Pasadèl at the Grand Gala: the unexpected stepback, the Scirea Hop instead of the sliding finale. He lifts himself from the ground and seems about to stumble again but instead rises into the air: the weightless man and his gamble.

I lift my hands from the edge of the table: I leave the cards where they were dealt and don't look at them. My pulse is stable, my head good, my legs cool. The seams of skin dry at the base of my fingers. And I feel it: the deck is tired.

'I'd like to be excused,' I say, getting up. I pull the chair away from the table, go to the coat rack, open the inside pocket of my coat and take the three thousand euros. I go back to the table and count out a thousand, lay it at my place: 'I'd like to be excused.'

'Like this?' the septuagenarian asks.

'Yes.'

'Leave like this?'

'Yes.' And I wait for them to excuse me. They do so with a nod of their heads, the last one to agree is Cardigan.

Then the septuagenarian gets up, comes to count my money, asks me to leave, and I leave. He walks me to the door and waits for me to step outside, to leave behind once and for all the villa of the three chimneys, and my own scaramàz.

Your dad: the man who flew at the Grand Gala. You should've seen their faces, Muccio. You should've seen their faces.

In 2008 he called Daniele and Walter and invited them over to the house: he wanted to understand. Lele warned me they were planning to go and at first it pissed me off, but then I got curious and asked them to report back to me right after.

I waited at my office desk, then I went out for a stroll down Corso Sempione, stopping for a coffee near the Arco della Pace, then I continued on towards Porta Romana, where I got a text from Walter: they were all still there and were going to have dinner together. What do you mean have dinner together? Have dinner together – we couldn't say no to your dad's cockerel cacciatore.

Them with cockerel cacciatore, me with an artichoke sandwich at Bar Quadronno, pretending to read the paper, still waiting, until more than an hour later they called me on speaker from the car: you're sending him to an early grave, Sandro, and Caterina too.

They explained that my mum came home in the middle of dinner, so they stopped talking about me, but then they started up again with her and she listened, acting as if she knew all of it better than anyone. It's settled, she finally said, worn down by that chorus he had wanted. And then they ate caramelised figs, a whole jarful, smearing them with goat ricotta and gradually lapsing into silence.

When I go back to the San Fortunato viewpoint, Lele is sitting on the low wall smoking. I leave my car next to his MiTo and sit down beside him.

He keeps smoking. 'Well then.'

'You know.'

'You gave it up.'

'I have to go see Bruni.'

'You really gave it up?'

'I need to make things right with Bruni.'

'He has a kid with a woman who doesn't like people coming over at night.'

'I have to see him before tomorrow.'

'You really gave it up.'

I start laughing.

'What the fuck are you laughing at, Sandro?'

'Your face when I showed up at the villa.'

'Arsehole.' He snuffs his cigarette and keeps the butt. 'And what did the other players say?'

'I didn't even look at my cards.'

'You didn't look?'

I shake my head.

'I can't believe you didn't look at them.'

'If you look you're playing.'

I never heard him say: you, Sandro, broke your mother's heart. You and your vice killed her.

Lele goes with me to Bruni's. He follows me in his car and waits at the end of the street. His apartment is in Marina Centro, facing the tennis courts.

I call and get no answer. I send a text and Bruni looks out from his balcony and signals for me to wait in my car. He comes down, gets in, and I pull out the two thousand euros and hand them to him.

He takes them. 'They warned me.'

'I'm done.'

He fiddles with his house keys. His red face is covered by a beard.

'Sorry for the trouble.'

'You'll end up in casinos and online games.'

I shake my head. 'You know I only like small groups.'

We're quiet, and I know he's smiling even though he's looking away.

'What about your gift, Sandro?'

'You made it up.'

Now he turns and stares at me. He still has the money in his fist, lifts his pelvis to stick it in his trouser pocket. 'Don't call me again.' Clicks the roof of his mouth.

And the applause at the Baia Imperiale? So much applause, Muccio. And your dad? He was so light. Light? He was floating, even as we left the dance floor. And later too: floating up there.

And then we walk, Lele and I, leaving the cars on Bruni's street. We walk at a fast clip past the anchor memorial and down the length of the Palata as it stretches into the sea, with the fog surprising us at the rocky tip. Separating us.

'Hey, still there?' I ask.

He grabs my arm and we agree we can't wait for Walter because it's freezing. We call him to tell him but he's already at the marina. When he arrives we're sitting by the yellow beacon.

'That you, muppets?'

'Who else.'

'Damn, you're ugly,' he says as he sits, a curly-headed mushroom, beside us. We huddle like we did at the stellario, only now Lele is in the middle. We fasten our coat collars, the beacon flashes, and the fog is Rimini blowing smoke in our faces.

'I've got the definitive answer for the extra million.' Walter scoots away from us. 'A boat. We dock it at the Palata and sell fried fish for lunch and go out to sea in the evenings.'

'I get seasick,' says Lele.

'Jesus, this guy gets seasick too.' Walter stands and the beacon blinds him. 'Think about it.'

'You've got quite a bit left over.'

'Nah, that guy blew it at the card table.' Pointing at me. We laugh.

'What about the twenty years younger?'

'What do we need to be twenty years younger for, us.'

Twenty years younger and I'm at the Rimini train station – late September. Lele is there too and we're about to take the regional train to Bologna. The next day we're starting our third year of university.

We have one suitcase apiece and a third with sheets and cutlets and our mothers' sauces. He has accompanied us to the platform as he does at the start of every academic term. 'Take care,' he says when we're about to board the train.

Then we pull away, watching him through the window, as he stands there waving at us with his car keys in his hand. Twenty years ago: what more could I have said to him, what more.

'That you love him,' Bibi says. 'What else can you say to a father.' She matches her gait to mine and we keep in step from Piazza Cavour to Ponte di Tiberio. We get out of sync and I regain my long stride. We've made a habit of walking from Ina Casa to the sea through the historic centre, returning by way of the park.

'I wanted to tell him I do have a bit of him in me.' We're entering Borgo San Giuliano. 'A bit of what he gave me.'

'But he knew that.'

'I don't know if he did.'

'He definitely did.'

'He knew I was different.'

'Like all children.'

I smile. 'Different as in messed up.'

'Messed up.'

'The apple that fell far from the tree.'

She knots her scarf. 'C'mon, keep moving.'

And I see she's walking faster, almost trotting, and the effort to keep up pushes my thoughts aside, and she senses it, and by the end of the neighbourhood she's pleased with herself for having chased my gloom away. Then we come, emptied of everything, to the water piazza, the Ponte di Tiberio reflected in it, its arches like soaking circles. It's cold as hell and Bibi slows down: 'And besides, we like messed up.'

Not having checked my cards before leaving the table at the villa of the three chimneys in Covignano: that chance that I had been dealt a pair, two pair, trips.

Don Paolo shows up at the house early in the morning, rings the bell. He's decked out for the North Pole: hood, gloves, scarf around his face. All I can see of him are his eyebrows, which he rubs as he waits at the gate, battered by the tramontana. I ask him to come in even though he wants to walk. He agrees and defrosts at the bottom of the stairs, but in the hall he becomes wary, afraid of making a mess with his shoes. I slip off his jacket and unwrap his scarf.

'You don't want to come for a quick walk, Sandro?'

'Come to the living room.'

He doesn't move.

'Come to the living room.'

We move together, tentatively, and he's looking around until I hand him the bag with the LPs Nando left him. He looks through them, Guccini and a dozen others, and after careful thought pulls one out. 'Put this on.'

It's Jimmy Fontana, *Il mondo*. I go to the record player and put it on even though around here it got played every Sunday morning. We listen with bowed heads to three-fourths of a song, then I look up and for the first time see a priest cry.

They met on 22 November 1970, at a dance hall in Milano Marittima. Caterina was with her friends, Nando was with his, and before he could ask her to dance the evening began winding down.

She was about to leave, and he still needed time to boost his courage. He made do without, and approaching the small sofa where she was sitting, he extended a hand and asked: 'May I invite you to dance, miss?'

I bet 210,450 euros. I lost 122,470 euros.

I wake to a cloud-streaked sky and persimmons swinging from their branches. I open the window and sniff the tramontana. The garden looks sandy and the vine shoots are charcoal knots. I make tea and eat fruitcake and stand and watch as Sabatini pulls bags of topsoil from his Panda. He unloads them one at a time, carries them around the back and stacks them next to the cauliflower patch. The day after the funeral he offered to keep the garden going for me until tomato season. He also took care of the Christmas lights: the day before yesterday he put white ones on the fig and the acacia, blue ones on the wooden shed and the three pomegranates.

I take a sweatshirt from the wardrobe and pull it on over my sweater. Still cold, I put on my coat and check that my hat is in the pocket. I grab the keys and go downstairs, into the garage. The Renault 5 is parked next to the seven boxes I've kept, the ones with his Sunday-best jackets, sweaters and shirts. I go into the adjoining laundry room; I've piled dirty clothes on the ironing board. I put a load of darks into the washing machine and start it, set up the clothesline between the water heater and her canvases.

'The paintings won't get wrecked by the heat, right, Nando?'

'Gimme a break.' He had catalogued them by year and subject.

I pull out the nearest one, peel the plastic off: it's the kneeling juniper from Piscinas beach in Sardinia. The patches of colour on one of the branches: the bathing suits we'd hang there after swimming. I set it aside on top of the dresser, making room for it behind the box with the inkwells, next to the Grand Gala poster.

I open the garage doors and the gate and get into the Renault 5, close the garage and gate again after pulling out on to Via Magellano, then I head south down a wide avenue towards the hills, opening the window a bit: the tramontana is blowing the salt air away and bringing the smell of woodsmoke in from the countryside.

I take the bypass, a blocked artery where the city ends, this land whose passage into the cold resembles a respite:

the tired light, the people and objects becoming themselves again as summer recedes. I leave the bypass and leave Rimini, the sun now high, and the closer I get to Montescudo the wilder the land becomes.

I turn on the radio, change stations: none is playing a song I want to hear. The three of us used to play a sort of game: we'd each name a song then turn the dial five times hoping to hear one of them. She was the only one who ever managed it, but it didn't count because Enrico Ruggeri had won Sanremo the day before. He wouldn't count it and neither would I.

The air gets warm as I enter Montescudo. The cobblestoned street splits the village in two, and I follow the ridge out of town until the turn that leads into the hills. I climb and take the gravel road just past the field. The farmhouse is half-hidden by acacias and walnuts, its façade pink stone fading to white under the roof. Once, to deter thieves after someone cut his fence, he put a 'Video Surveillance Area' sign up there along with a fake camera. It didn't happen again, which he bragged about, and every time he passed under the camera he looked up in an unnatural way.

I open the big gate and park in the flat area where he used to set up his table in spring. Someone was always visiting him – Don Paolo, former colleagues. Or else he would eat alone on the veranda, which offers a glimpse of the Adriatic.

I walk up the slope, pausing at the row of olives that ends with the cherry tree. In the overgrown area, ivy has climbed the five hazels and spread a thick, rumpled mantle over the ground. He always left it alone – the only place he didn't venture into with his strimmer. She begged him not to: and spare the wildflowers too, please. He who would leave one sliver untrimmed and later buzz that too.

Past the ivy the slope flattens: a broad square where they said they would put a ping-pong table. Then one day they brought a stone here from the ruined church. He used chisel and sandpaper, she painted eyes, and out came a stone porcupine.

The porcupine gazes towards the fence, half sunken, eyes faded, back retaken by moss. Around it: the frog, the boar they claimed was a hare, and seven other animals – including three he added after she died. They're the ones that aren't painted. The last one is a blunt-billed buzzard. Tamping with my soles, I smooth the earth around each of them. Then I go to the rainwater basins, get the bucket and mop, and return to the animals. I squat down and start cleaning. When I'm done, the water has turned them dark.

'The animal cemetery,' he said.

'But they're alive,' she replied.

'So, Animal Hill.'

'Animal Hill.'

I go down to the tool shed, twenty metres below, look for the rock we took from the church. It's under the over-turned wheelbarrow and the ivy. To exhume it I grab the sides, fingers digging into the mud, and plant my feet to try to lift it, but I stop because it's too stuck. I look for a piece of wood, open the shed and find the pickaxe, start levering the rock up until I'm out of breath. Then I rest. Then I start again with the pickaxe until the rock is really free and I am calm.

I bend over and grab it and this time I manage to lift it up, lean it against my coat, and start walking up a little stretch of road and then another little stretch until my hands are burning and my back is straining and I come to Animal Hill. I place it between the buzzard and the boar, pointing the tip towards the Adriatic. He would have carved the head here.

Your turtle.